Tempting Turquoise

Amy Ruttan
Elaine Lowe
Regina Carlysle

ELLORA'S CAVE
ROMANTICA PUBLISHING

What the critics are saying…

୨୦

4.5 Rating "*Feral Moon* is a pleasurable Were-panther read that will heat-up any room. Regina Carlysle heats up the sheets with her sexy Were-panthers. If you are looking for a fun, sexy shifter novel you will enjoy this quickie from Ellora's Cave." ~ *Night Owl Romance Reviews*

An Ellora's Cave Romantica Publication

www.ellorascave.com

Tempting Turquoise

ISBN 9781419958755
ALL RIGHTS RESERVED.
Rain God Copyright © 2008 Amy Ruttan
Feral Moon Copyright © 2008 Regina Carlysle
Veins of Turquoise Copyright © 2008 Elaine Lowe
Edited by Shannon Combs and Helen Woodall.
Cover art by Syneca.

This book printed in the U.S.A. by Jasmine-Jade Enterprises, LLC.

Trade paperback Publication March 2009

With the exception of quotes used in reviews, this book may not be reproduced or used in whole or in part by any means existing without written permission from the publisher, Ellora's Cave Publishing, Inc.® 1056 Home Avenue, Akron OH 44310-3502.

Warning: The unauthorized reproduction or distribution of this copyrighted work is illegal. Criminal copyright infringement, including infringement without monetary gain, is investigated by the FBI and is punishable by up to 5 years in federal prison and a fine of $250,000.
(http://www.fbi.gov/ipr/)

This book is a work of fiction and any resemblance to persons, living or dead, or places, events or locales is purely coincidental. The characters are productions of the author's imagination and used fictitiously.

TEMPTING TURQUOISE

RAIN GOD
Amy Ruttan
~11~

FERAL MOON
Regina Carlysle
~59~

VEINS OF TURQUOISE
Elaine Lowe
~101~

RAIN GOD
Amy Ruttan

%

Chapter One
America, 2100 A.D.

Shana held up the turquoise to the bright desert light. The blues were so rich and deep in this stone. The blue-green color was like the mythical oceans of long ago, as it refracted the red sand and stone of the buttes and mesas that surrounded her and her surveillance dig.

"Beautiful," she whispered to herself as she twirled it between her dusty, slender fingers. Goose bumps traveled up her arm as the words slipped past her lips. *Try to focus Shana. You're not here to marvel at old relics, you're here for water.* She was head of water reconnaissance for this sector of the world.

When she had been growing up she had heard tales from her great-grandmother about how the world had been covered with water, and that there were two great caps of ice that covered the top and the bottom of the Earth. Such a wondrous vision, it had inspired Shana to strive to become the head of water reconnaissance for the American desert land. The hunt for the precious commodity was the most thrilling, exciting job for a young person fresh out the Interstellar Academy.

Save our dying world. It was the motto she lived by. It paid her well, she got the most water rations than any other job she could have pursued in the Academy and it allowed her to travel and explore the flat desert plains.

She just wished that she could find water.

Shana shook her head, she tucked the turquoise stone into her pouch and zipped it up so she wouldn't lose it.

"Commander Kelley."

Shana looked over her shoulder, flipping her visor back down in place. It was strictly forbidden to expose your eyes to the overbright sun in the desert plains. It could cause serious damage and the Interstellar Academy didn't want to take any risks with their water reconnaissance team. It was bullshit. She had been using her sight without her visor for years. It was the only way she could really survey the land. The only way she could find the ancient grooves that scarred the dry parched Earth. The grooves that told her water had once flowed there.

"Commander Kelley." The young cadet just fresh out of the Academy saluted and held himself rigidly at attention. "Ensign Johnson reporting for duty, Ma'am."

Smiling, she admired his tight physique in the body-hugging suit that protected him from the sun's heat and its radiation working on the desert plains. He was too young really for play. She had no time for that.

Shana stood up and circled the young ensign, asserting her power over him as commander. Just as her commander had done to her twelve years ago when she had been eighteen and fresh out of the Academy.

"At ease, Ensign Johnson. What do you have to report?"

"An entrance to an underground cave. Lieutenant Meyers thinks that it could lead to a possible mythical underground water source."

A smile tugged at Shana's lips, *this is just what I need*. She never dreamed, never hoped that she would ever find one of the entrances to the mysterious caverns that contained underground lakes. Another one of her great-grandmother's myths about ancient times, just like the story how the past timers would actually bathe in the water.

Water had been that abundant. Shana found it hard to believe.

"Take me to him, Ensign, and if this is true I'll have you promoted to lieutenant in no time."

Ensign Johnson tried to suppress his smile as he saluted her again. "Thank you, Commander. This way, if you please."

Suppressing a giggle, she followed the exuberant ensign down the craggy hill in the shadow of a mesa toward the midpoint of the plane that they had been surveying. She could see through her zoom visors that her lieutenant had staked out something around the outcropping of a crumbling past timer village.

When she approached Lieutenant Meyers, he saluted her.

"At ease, what have you found?"

"A crack in the surface, but not just any kind of crack, it's a passageway. It looks like it has been carved by past timers."

A tingle ran down Shana's spine as she stepped around her lieutenant and hit the button on the side of her visor to zoom in the small opening that was marked.

"Indeed," she murmured to herself as she inspected the lieutenant's find. The zoom on her visor allowed her to inspect the deep dark cavern, or what appeared to be a cavern.

It did look like the walls were carved, that it wasn't erosion or the shifting plates of the Earth that had formed the passageway. Her heart beat faster as she zoomed as far as she could. It seemed to go on forever, deep into the heart of the Earth. *Maybe this is it.*

She stepped back, smiling and nodding solemnly. "Good job, Lieutenant, we'll send a robot in to follow the passageway to determine if there is any water."

"Why don't we just set charges and blast the passageway open?" Ensign Johnson blurted out.

Leveling her most stern disapproving look, she put the young ensign in his place. Crossing her arms, she looked down at the quaking man. She'd give him a break this time.

"Why don't we set charges to blast the passageway open, Lieutenant Meyers?" Shana asked, keeping her gaze locked on the trembling ensign.

"So that any water that is in the crack won't evaporate when it hits the air on the surface," Lieutenant Meyers responded. Shana heard the smug satisfaction in his voice. Meyers certainly liked to show off.

"That's why, Ensign. You'd best learn that, or you'll cost your people a precious commodity, is that understood?" Shana said, watching as the ensign saluted, nodding his head vehemently.

"Yes, Commander Kelley." Ensign Johnson nervously licked his dry lips and saluted. A distant sound of thunder rolled in the distance. Scanning the horizon, she could see the dark violent electric clouds rolling across the mesa.

"Time to go." Turning to her lieutenant, she signaled for him to sound the alarm. "Have the team return to their pods."

"Aye," Lieutenant Meyers saluted before turning on his heel and marching away. Ensign Johnson followed in Meyer's footsteps.

Shana sighed, an electric storm was something you couldn't be caught in. That's why man hadn't lived on the Earth in more than a century. Instead he lived in space in a network of stations that hovered what was once a lush and verdant planet.

She unzipped her pouch and pulled out the precious stone. She should toss it back to the dust and leave it where she found it. It was just a useless mineral. She shouldn't keep it, they weren't really supposed to take things from the Earth. It was a reserve, a historic site. They were trying to restore an ecosystem and anything removed or misplaced could upset the balance.

Palming it, she turned to toss it, but stopped herself. She held the turquoise up against the dark sky, admiring the dark blue hue it took on, as if it were swallowing the storm. *Keep it*, a little voice said in the back of her mind.

"Commander Kelley, we're ready to depart."

Turning back, she saw that Lieutenant Meyers was holding the last pod for her. The rest of her team already rising back toward the station, she nodded and slipped the stone back into the pouch on the side of her tight jumpsuit.

One little mineral, one little gem from a dead planet wouldn't be missed by anyone. Would it?

* * * * *

Shana rubbed her tired eyes and clicked off the computer monitor in her quarters. She stretched her back before she pulled the tight suit off her body. Padding over to the incinerator, she jammed her suit into the unit and recycled her contaminated uniform.

Arching her back, she stretched once more before stepping naked into the solar shower. She allowed the rays to decontaminate her body. It only took a few moments before the system announced she was spic-and-span.

"Please select the attire," the computer voice chimed. Biting her lip, she was about to select a simple sleep uniform, but then thought better. She selected no attire and stepped out of the solar shower naked.

"Lights, music," she said as the computer dimmed the lights and opened the shutter so she could have a nice view of the moon as the station orbited. The sound of rain filtered through her sound system.

The pitter-pattering that she had never actually heard softly filtered through the speakers. It always put her to sleep, the gentle drum of the rain. It was the stuff of dreams. She hoped one day the scientists would figure out a way to restore the delicate ecosystem and that she would see rain in her lifetime.

It had been her mother's dream and her mother's before her. She caught sight of the turquoise glinting on her desk near her computer monitor. It sparkled in the dim light the moon was casting through her small window.

Smiling, she closed her eyes and began to drift to sleep. She dreamed of rain, of water falling from the sky.

* * * * *

Warm rain washed over her body, making her hair wet. Something she could only imagine. It pattered over her like silk, soft, wet. Her body was slick as she ran her hands over her skin.

The sensation caused her pussy to become wet. It turned her on letting something so natural and pure run over her.

Opening her eyes, she saw that the rain was purple and blue as it washed over the scarred landscape of the Earth. It caused the cracks to seam together, like a needle to a thread.

Then she sensed him, a dream lover, turning she saw him standing through the downpour. His eyes were dark and glowing as he stared at her. She wanted him. She wanted him in the rain.

The man stepped forward. His eyes were pitch black as he approached her. The water was running in rivulets over his body. There was a crack of thunder and a bolt of lightning that seemed to cause his eyes to glow like a dark fire.

Moving like quicksilver, he pressed his body against hers. He ran his fingers over her cheeks before his hard strong hands ran through her silken hair, pulling her forward so that he could capture her lips with his mouth. His hot, wet tongue invaded her mouth, entwining with hers as he kissed her deeply.

Moaning, she pressed her body tighter against his, the water making their skin slick. She could feel his cock hard against her belly and she could feel her cream between her thighs. His body was hard, hot and taut, she wanted him so badly. She wanted to fuck him.

As if reading her mind he broke off the kiss and let his hand trail down her body, his fingers parting her folds to rub her clit.

"Oh God," she cried out, throwing her head back. She let the rain wash over her face and down her neck. Warm like a caress.

His hands slipped around her waist and down to her ass, cupping her cheeks. He lifted her up and positioned himself. She wrapped her legs around his waist and could feel the hard head of his cock rubbing up and down the slit of her cunt. Arching her hips forward, he entered her swiftly, burying his shaft deep inside her.

Shana snaked her arms around his neck and clutched his muscular shoulder blades. Burying her face in his neck, she inhaled his spicy, musky scent. He kneaded the cheeks of her ass and began to pump in and out of her. Raising her up and sliding her down the length of his cock. Grinding her hips, she matched his rhythm, with each sure stroke he built up the tension inside her. Her nipples puckered and she felt his hot mouth on them, laving each sensitive peak as he began to fuck her faster.

Her blood coursed through her veins like liquid fire, the water was steaming as it hit her skin. Her body was so tense and she could feel herself on the verge of releasing. She felt as if she were going to shatter into a million pieces.

Digging her nails into his copper skin, she cried out as her pussy clenched around his shaft when she came fast and hard. He grunted as he released.

Breathing heavy, she looked at him, his black eyes piercing hers, seeming to delve deep into her soul.

"Why have you brought me here?" he asked, his voice booming like thunder.

* * * * *

Crying out, she sat up abruptly in bed. Startled she had thought she heard his voice so clearly, so loudly.

"Why have you brought me here?" he said again, this time Shana knew that it wasn't a dream.

Her heart began to beat wildly and she shivered in the dim light of her room. Her eyes adjusted, but it just couldn't be right. Her senses were definitely playing a trick on her, and a mean one at that.

Standing a few feet from her was a massive man. Massive only in height and by the breadth of his rock-hard chest and muscular shoulders.

His skin was the color of copper. Like the color of the rich vibrant buttes that dotted the dead, dry desert plains. Shana had never seen a skin color like it before, it almost seemed as if he were on fire, almost. An intricate tattoo surrounded his right eye over his thick black brow.

He was tall too. No man was built like that. Hell, she had never seen a man who stood over six feet. He had to be at least six foot two, maybe three. His hair hung in black waves, thick, to his shoulders. His eyes were just as dark, keen and perceptive like a bird of prey. They were as dark as the electric thunderheads that covered most of the northern desert plains and the hollows of the great sea.

Call for a code, her logical inner voice told her. *Call for help,* but she was frozen, trapped and held in awe by him.

"Who are you?" she finally asked.

"I'm T'koh, why have you brought me here?" His voice was deep and booming.

"I didn't bring you here," Shana said, sitting upright. She watched as his gaze flickered lower and she heard a growl of appreciation escape his mouth. Looking down, she remembered that she was naked and very aroused from her brief dream.

"I see why you have summoned me. It has been many sleeps since I have been asked to mate with a woman." He loosened the animal skin that was wrapped around his waist. She watched in stunned silence as it dropped to the floor, in its wake it revealed the largest cock she had ever seen.

Rain God

It caused her to become wet with arousal. She had been with finest male specimens of the Interstellar Academy — human and alien alike — but none compared to the stranger standing before her.

T'koh took a step closer. She could smell his arousal and it jarred her back to reality.

"I'm not here to mate with you," she said breathlessly. It almost killed her to say it when her body was screaming for her to shut up.

"Who are you?" he asked.

"I'm Commander Shana Kelley."

T'koh frowned and looked confused. "I do not understand. Why was I summoned then?"

"I told you, I didn't summon you," Shana said again trying to tear her gaze from his cock, which was still standing at attention.

"You must have," he growled, crossing his thick arms. "I am summoned to mate with the chosen one during times of drought. I make the water come."

"Excuse me?" Shana sputtered.

"The stone," he said, nodding his head back toward her desk where the turquoise gem glittered beside her darkened monitor. "It knows when the right mate is chosen for me. I am summoned and with our joining, I make the water come."

"Water?" she asked feeling her throat tighten with that thought. Her pulse raced and her head spun. He couldn't mean water, it didn't exist anymore. Not in vast quantities anyways. "Water?" she asked again trying to reassure that she heard him correctly.

"Yes," he said unsurely. "Do you not know who I am?"

Shana shook her head slowly.

Rolling his eyes, he put his hands on his hips. "I'm T'koh, god of water, god of rain. I make the water come."

Chapter Two

※

"Standard dress," Shana said brusquely, pushing the said "god of water" into the solar shower and shutting him in the small stall. After his appearance she had jumped into the solar shower and had a standard issue suit put on. Putting on the tight suit did nothing to soothe his ardor.

"What is the name of...ack!"

Giggling, she heard his high-pitched squeal. Once the solar shower was complete, he walked out in a skintight jumpsuit that was standard issue for occupants of the space station.

T'koh's face paled and he looked none too impressed.

"I do not like that," he said emphatically, stabbing his finger in the direction of the shower booth.

"You'll get used to it."

"And what is this midnight skin it has attached to me?" he asked in disgust, pulling at the tight-fitting fabric.

"It's..."she trailed off as she admired his form in the standard issue jumpsuit. It hugged him like a second skin indeed. Every rock-hard muscle, every curve was amplified in the jumpsuit.

It wasn't only the muscles that were being shown off. What she had spied earlier was just as prominent as when he was naked.

"I see that you appreciate me clothed in the midnight skin," he said, smiling and flashing her brilliant white teeth. "Then that is all that matters, I shall wear it to please you, *Ne-Zhoni.*"

She had no idea what he was saying, but whatever it was, it sounded good. He stepped closer to her. He had the most intense, earthy smell to him. Something exotic and forgotten, something about him excited her to her very core. He could be anyone, really.

He could be a member of the Hazoor faction. A faction who believed that Earth should not be restored, but harvested for what pressure minerals and alloys remained, the Hazoor were a constant threat to their missions. Security officials had not yet tracked down the ringleader of the faction, he could be their leader.

"Whoa there, buddy," she said, holding up a hand. "Just step back a bit."

He looked at her confused. "Buddy? What is this buddy, and why should I step back from you, *Ne-Zhoni*? You are my chosen mate. We need to be closer to make the rain come."

A delicious chill traveled down her spine again as she thought about *mating* with him. The thought was appealing, whether he was a member of the Hazoor faction or not, she wanted him and bad.

"Look, guy, I am a commander of Water Recon. I can't be fooled by this malarkey. What faction are you with?" She backed herself against the wall where she had access to call a code. "If you tell me what faction you're with it will make things a lot easier."

"You speak nonsense, *Ne-Zhoni*."

Shana didn't have time to react, it seemed he moved like lightning across the expanse of her quarters and she was pressed up against him, her body molding against the hard planes of his chest. His body was like a flame through the jumpsuit. She could feel herself melting in his arms, her knees going weak as he held her.

T'koh's arms slid down her back to her rear. "Perhaps I do like this midnight skin," he whispered into her ear. His hands cupping her ass, pulling her flush against his loins so that she could feel his hard cock pressing against her stomach.

Shana stared up at him, his eyes were flinty like the electric clouds that swept across the mesas. They were dark and full of life, an electric spark like none she had ever seen before. It seemed as if his eyes burned like the electrical storms on Earth, there was something magical and mysterious about him.

Letting out a sigh, she closed her eyes, waiting for him to lean in and kiss her. She did not have long to wait before his lips brushed against hers. At first so lightly, a kiss like butterfly wings beating against her, and then it deepened, intensified as if he were trying to devour her, and she wanted to be devoured so *badly*.

His tongue pushed past her lips, entwining with hers. Giving in, she slid her hands around his neck and let her fingers run through his silky black hair. Her nipples hardened under the jumpsuit, and his hands kneaded her ass and pulled her in tight against his erection.

Breaking off the kiss, he began to nibble her ear and down her neck, his hands sliding up her body to cup her breast. His thumbs brushed against her hardened nipples, closing her eyes she moaned. Her pussy was so wet with need. She wanted out of the tight suit and wanted him on the bed so she could ride him.

"I think that we need to leave your *hogan* and go to the heart to mate," he said huskily in her ear.

Before she had time to react he scooped her up and was heading to the door. The cabin door opened, sensing her presence. It slid open with a hiss and he carried her into the hallway.

"What in the name of Creator is this?" He put her down, his face pale and his body shaking. Shana bit her lip. Being a commander of the Water Recon team afforded her many luxuries, including quarters on *The Causeway,* an opulent space ship that was permanently docked at the space station to give officers the very best in accommodations. *The Causeway* was mostly made of observation decks, which meant her entrance had a clear uninterrupted view of Earth as the station orbited.

"Have you never seen the Earth before?"

"That is Earth, and we are in the heavens?" he asked in confusion, walking across the observation deck to press his face against the glass and stare at the brown scarred planet below them. He looked back at her. "That is not Earth. Where is the water?"

"There is none," Shana said incredulously. "Look, shouldn't you know all of this? I mean it's common knowledge, even for the Hazoor."

Shaking his head, T'koh touched the glass, staring in wonder. "I do not know what you speak of. Is this Hazoor some kind of warring tribe? Did they do this to the Earth?"

Cocking her head to one, she stared in wonder. "You really don't know do you? I mean, you really believe you are this rain god you claim to be."

T'koh uncrossed his arms and stood akimbo, staring down at her. "I have told you, I am T'koh. I make the rain come."

A shiver ran down her spine. She should have never picked up that turquoise. She should've left it in the sand of the American plains. Running her hands through her red curls, she stared out at the vastness of space, the stars and distant galaxies glittering out in space.

She had seen a lot of weird things during her years at the Academy, so why was it so hard to believe that this man standing in front of her was indeed an ancient god. *You doubt it because it seems too easy, and you know it.*

"Where am I?" T'koh finally asked. "What has happened to Mother Earth? Why has Father Sky forsaken her?"

Biting her lip, she looked up at him, his brow creased in concern. "The water dried up approximately a century ago."

"How many moons is a century?"

Of course he would ask something like that. Flipping open her wristband she typed in the equation into her computer. T'koh stared in wonder at it as the answer flashed up on the tiny screen.

"So what does the bracelet say? How many moons in this century you speak?"

"One thousand, two hundred and fifty-nine moons."

T'koh took a couple of steps back and then ran his hand through his black hair. "Why was I not summoned earlier?"

"That's a good question," Shana said, tapping her chin thoughtfully. "When was the last time you were summoned?"

"I believe the last mate that I took was when the white man came to the scarred lands between the four mountains."

"The four mountains?"

"Yes," T'koh said, turning and looking back at the Earth and frowning. "That is where the heart is located, the heart of Mother Earth. There I can make the rain come."

"What do you do when you are not summoned? Where do you go?"

"Go?" he asked, cocking an eyebrow. "I close my eyes, and then I awake…here."

"Your spirit is connected to the turquoise?"

"Aye," he nodded, smiling at her. "But there have been other times of drought since the white man came to the land of the four mountains. This is what puzzles me, why was no mate chosen? Why was I not summoned?"

"That is a quandary," Shana said. "Maybe you were lost. You said you were kept in the heart, was the heart a cavern in the Earth?"

"Aye, deep in the Earth where the water flows eternally."

She didn't have the heart to tell him not anymore. "I didn't find you in a cavern, I found you buried in the Earth, next to a ruined village carved in the side of a butte."

"Then I was lost in that battle," T'koh turned his back. "I do not like seeing Mother Earth this way, devoid of life. I mourn her, the animals, the plants. Please, is there somewhere we can go?"

Taking his large rough hand in hers, she squeezed it and smiled. "There's somewhere else that may make you feel better."

* * * * *

"By the Creator," T'koh said in wonder as they walked in the space stations arboretum.

Shana smiled as she watched him wander into the natural habitat that was orbiting the Earth. The arboretum was huge, it sustained each distinct ecosystem of Earth. The animals were housed in another habitat on another section of the ship. This arboretum housed a delicate balance of plant life that they sustained in the hopes of replanting it on the Earth. The only life forms that inhabited this arboretum were insects of the pollen spreading variety, the butterflies, the bees, that kind of thing, all of which were monitored strictly so that the balance could be kept. It was little pockets of artificial ecosystems like these that were the foundation of the Hazoor's mantra. Why replant a dead world when that world could be sustained in space?

Why indeed, because as far as Shana was concerned it was not natural. That is why she joined the Interstellar Academy. The need to save the Earth and restore it to its ancient glory.

"This is like paradise," T'koh said in wonder as he bent over a hot pink orchid and delicately touched the petals. "Such wonders I have never seen."

Shana smacked her forehead. He would have been used to the desert ecosystem, not the pacific rainforest.

"Such trees," T'koh said, touching the bark of a tall tree. "Such things I have not seen."

"It's beautiful isn't it?"

"You have preserved Mother Earth?" A smiled tugged at the corner of his lips, his eyes were sparkling. "This is remarkable."

"It's my job. One day, when we figure out how to bring water to the world again we'll reseed the Earth so that we can live there once more."

"We shall make it so when we mate in the heart." He sent her a look that caused a jolt of electricity to surge through her. "For now, we can mate here and I can show you exactly how I make Mother Earth…wet."

Shana's mouth went dry as he peeled the jumpsuit off his body. The fake sunlight of the arboretum caused his copper skin to glow like an ember. Looking over her shoulder, she checked the observation room and saw that it was empty. Flipping open her wrist computer, she punched in a code and put the arboretum in a lockdown.

"Commander?" A voice came over the intercom. It was Ensign Maxwell, another fresh face from the Interstellar Academy. "You've put habitat thirty-five on lockdown, is everything okay?"

"Aye, Ensign, there's been a small leak, a one-man job. I have a tech down here with me and we're rectifying the situation." She eyed T'koh slyly as he stepped toward her, she could feel the cream between her legs, hot and wet as she eyed his large cock that rose from the dark curls of his loins. How she wanted to taste that cock, run her tongue down the side of it. "I discovered the leak on a routine check. We're taking care of it. Until then habitat thirty-five is on lockdown, keep the scientists at bay until the security is cleared."

"I'm not sensing a leak."

"Ensign," she said warningly. "How many leaks in habitation have you dealt with since you left the Academy?"

There was a pause on the other end and then a defeated sigh. "None, Commander."

"I thought so, put habitat thirty-five on lockdown. If I require back up, I'll call."

"Aye-aye."

The com went out and she flipped shut her wrist band. The Ensign closed the habitation off from prying eyes, big shutters descending from the ceiling, closing them off as lockdown was put into place.

"Shall I help you out of your midnight skin?" he asked as he ran his hands down her body.

"Oh God, yes," she whispered.

T'koh grabbed hold of the zipper at the front of her uniform and tugged it slowly, ending just below her bellybutton. He pushed the uniform off her shoulders, baring her breasts.

"Do you want to know how I make the Mother Earth wet?" he asked getting on his knees.

"Yes," she said. "Please, yes." *What are you doing?* Raking her hands through her red curls, she ignored her sense of reason for once. She had never done anything like this. Sex with a complete stranger, a man who claimed he was an ancient god of the Earth. A man who claimed to come from the turquoise that sat in her quarters.

When she was a cadet on deep space missions, leave meant one thing, sex and letting loose. At least that's what all her other comrades did—she didn't. On leave, she stayed locked up in her shared quarters, which would be empty, and study. That's how she got into Water Recon. That's why at the age of thirty she was a commander and not a lieutenant.

Since T'koh appeared, she had been attracted to him, and he was attracted to her. She didn't care if he claimed to be a god and she didn't care if he was a Hazoor insurgent. At this moment she only wanted one thing from him.

There was a slight rustle, she looked down and watched him as he began to tug the material from the rest of her body. She stepped out of the suit so that she was standing totally naked in front of him. He put his hands on her hips and she took a deep breath as she looked at him. His face, his mouth just inches from her pussy.

"By the Creator, I can see all of you."

Shana blushed. Standard Interstellar Academy cleanliness, hair on the backs, legs, underarms, chests and lower extremities were removed.

"It fires my blood. I can smell your arousal. You want me." He began to kiss her hips. "Do you want me?"

I do, she thought to herself. *Even though it's totally irrational and very unlike me to fuck a stranger.*

"What is irrational?" he murmured as he continued to kiss her.

Shana gasped. He had read her thoughts. She hadn't said that out loud. She was going to ask him how he had done that, how he had read her thoughts. That was until she felt his lips on her slit. His tongue was wet, hot and moist as it ran down one side of her labia and up the other.

"Oh God," she murmured, running her hand up to cup her breast.

"That's right, *Ne-Zhoni,* touch yourself." He chuckled huskily. He parted her labia and ran his tongue down her pussy, finding her clit. "You taste so good," T'koh murmured, running his tongue around the pearl of her pleasure.

Shana ran her fingers through his silken black hair. Her body felt so alive with the feel of his tongue lapping at her clit. Her blood thickened and she felt as if she were on fire as he tasted her. His hand slipped around her waist to cup her ass, kneading her cheeks, bringing her closer to his mouth.

Moaning, she moved her hips, angling her pussy against his tongue. The ball of tension, of absolute pleasure building deep within her belly, she was close and he knew it.

"Get on your knees, *Ne-Zhoni.* Let me take you," he murmured huskily against her belly.

Not arguing, she dropped to her knees. Shana reacted to the soft grass under her bare flesh. She had never fully reveled in the feeling of grass against her skin. The arboretums were usually full of scientists hovering around, and she had always been too self-conscious to take time to become one with nature in such an intimate way.

Now, here on her hands and knees, she felt the softness of the grass. The feel of moist earth that grass grew in, it was so exciting, so freeing. T'koh knelt behind her, and she looked over her shoulder to watch him as he put his copper-colored hands on her white ass, kneading her cheeks.

"Close your eyes and feel it come," he said, his voice hitching in his throat. "Let the water come."

"Just fuck me," she moaned thrusting her ass at him. "Just do it."

T'koh leaned over her back, his muscular arms splayed on either side of her body. "Feel," he whispered into her red hair. "Just feel the nature around you."

Swallowing hard, she nodded and closed her eyes, concentrating on the softness of the grass, the grains of soil rubbing against her skin, under her fingertips. Then the dream came, the feel of rain washing over her, cleansing her.

Shana felt his cock slide into her wet, tight sheath. It was so large it filled her and stretched her like she had never felt before.

"Oh God," she cried out, biting her lips.

"By Creator, you're tight." She heard him moan as he buried himself to the hilt.

T'koh held onto her hips, stilling her movements. All she wanted to do at that moment was buck up against him, she wanted to ride him.

"*Ne-Zhoni*, if you keep moving like that I will not last much longer." His voice was strained.

Tossing her hair over her shoulder, she peeked at him. His muscular body strained for control, his head thrown back, his neck corded and his muscles rippling as he held her there.

"Please," she panted, begging him to give it to her.

"By Creator," he cursed and he began to move slowly in and out of her, so that she moved up and down his hard, long, thick cock.

Biting her lip, she closed her eyes and concentrated on the feel of him moving inside her. Her breasts bouncing against her chest as he took her. Squeezing her Kegel muscle, she heard him moan. A secret smile tugged at the corner of her lips.

T'koh groaned and stilled her. "I will make this more difficult, *Ne-Zhoni*, if you continue to do this."

"Is that supposed to be a threat, Rain God?" she teased as she squeezed her muscles around his cock.

Growling, he grasped her hips and began to thrust into her at a blinding pace.

"Oh my God," she cried out as he fucked her like a wild stallion. Thrusting quickly, the pleasure building up inside her belly.

Shana heard him lick his fingers and then felt his hand slid under her and down her abdomen to her pussy. She bucked as the pads of his fingers began to rub at her clit in rapid circular motions.

The fire in her quickly spread to her loins. She grasped the grass between her fingers as he fucked her hard. Closing her eyes, she felt only him sliding in and out of her wetness.

A coil of pleasure unfurled in her body, and then she felt the mist against her back. She thought that water was being poured on her.

Crying out, she felt her orgasm start, her pussy clenching tight around his cock. She came fast and hard, and he followed right behind. She could hear him grunting as he released himself inside her.

Breathing heavy, she could still feel the water on her skin. He pulled himself away from her and she collapsed and rolled to her back, but something was not right. Her hair felt different, the grass under her back was moist. Gasping, she opened her eyes and looked at T'koh who was kneeling, his arms open, as he looked up at the ceiling of the arboretum.

"It's raining?" she said quizzically, watching the water fall from the dome. Her body was wet and her hair clung to her skin. It ran down in rivulets from his silken black hair and down his copper-colored torso. "It's really...I mean it's really water?"

Sitting up, she held out her hand, cupping it to catch the water. The rain began to dissipate as her hand filled with the precious clear liquid. Cool and shimmering, like diamonds in her palm.

Breathing heavy, her heart beating rapidly she brought the water up to her lips and tasted it. It was like nothing she had ever tasted before. It was so cold, so good.

Shana met his gaze as the water still dripped from his soaking wet locks of hair. His eyes were dark, intense. Like clouds after an electrical storm, empty but still capable of danger.

"How?" she whispered.

"I told you, I make the water come."

Chapter Three

The heat from the solar lamps and the preset temperature for the temperate zone that was being created soon evaporated any trace of the water that she and T'koh had created together.

Pulling on her jumpsuit, she still stared dumbfounded at the spot where they had; as T'koh put it, mated. The small patch of land where they had made it rain.

"When we mate in the heart the rain will come tenfold, it will heal Mother Earth."

"Are you certain?" Shana asked in disbelief. She knew that rain had never been recreated, even though the best scientists had the technology to recreate it. They knew how to recreate the water cycle. The problem was they did have not water to waste. If having sex with him in this heart place was the solution to the water problem, well, she was all for that. What a satisfying way to restore humanity.

Still she had her doubts. The scientist in her didn't believe what had just happened. She still had a hard time accepting that T'koh came from the piece of turquoise she had found.

"Are you not convinced?" he asked, holding out his hands.

Smiling, she zipped up her suit. "I'm convinced, but I need to find out more about the legend of your people."

T'koh nodded. "That is a wise course of action. The better you know the customs, the better chance we have of restoring the rain. We shall make Father Sky worship Mother Earth once more."

"You say the oddest things." Shana chuckled.

T'koh cocked his head to one side. "How is that odd? How is one's religion odd?"

"Touché," she quipped.

"What does that mean?"

"It's a French term in swordplay. It means 'to touch'."

Suddenly he was beside her, his hands cupping her cheeks. "I like touché, I like to touch you, *Ne-Zhoni*."

Leaning down, he kissed her, his lips brushing against her, his hot breath caressing her cheeks. Shana ran her hands through his still damp hair. Loving the feel of it running through her fingers, never had she felt wet hair before.

Even through her travels in the Interstellar Academy there had been no other planet such as Earth had been. No other glorious source of water had been discovered, no other planet out there. Most people her age had never had an experience such as she had just had. Shana was still in disbelief, having just felt water rain down on her, the feel of wet hair running across her skin, now wrapped up in his arms, she wanted him again. Drawing his face close, she nibbled on his lips. She wanted to make the rain come again, she wanted to get wet again. Really wet.

"Commander Kelley?"

Shana cursed, recognizing Lieutenant Meyer's voice. Looking over her shoulder, she saw that the arboretum had been opened once more and that Lieutenant Meyers and a couple of bleary-eyed ensigns were standing a few feet away from her.

"Is everything well, Commander Kelley? The ensign alerted me to the possibility of a leak."

Taking a deep breath to soothe the passion that had been stirred in her, she turned and faced her subordinates.

"Everything is fine, Lieutenant Meyers, although the lockdown should not have been released without my authority."

Meyer's eyes narrowed, his mouth a grim slash against his face. Shana was momentarily caught off guard by his reaction. She had never seen Meyer react in such a cold methodical way before.

"Well, when I did a routine scan of the arboretum I detected no leak. I thought you might have fixed it or…needed assistance," he said querulously, staring at T'koh standing behind her. "Who are you? What is your authorization, soldier?"

Crossing her arms, she glared right back at the lieutenant, she was no pushover. "He's not a soldier, he's a civilian and my guest."

Meyers sneered. "I don't recall any clearances about civilians in this sector of the station."

"I granted him clearance." Shana hoped that Meyers wouldn't go above her and check the log. She wouldn't have time to access the proper channels and fake the clearance. She held her breath, waiting for Meyers to accept her lie. For the life of her she couldn't figure out why he was acting so suspicious.

"Then that should be sufficient," Meyers said, clearing his throat. He looked past them. "So there's no leak?"

"A minor one that's been…contained, right now I am going to take Mr. Jansen here to the guest quarters."

"Who is this Jansen?" T'koh asked, tapping her on the shoulder.

Groaning, she grabbed his hand and pushed past Meyers and the sleepy ensigns. Meyers gave them a strange look as they passed. Shana was going to punish T'koh later for almost blowing their cover.

"I should very much like the form of punishment, especially if it involves blowing." T'koh whispered in her ear as the arboretum doors hissed shut behind them.

A blush crept up her cheeks at the thought of blowing and punishment filled her mind. Before she had a moment to relax, T'koh was pulling her into a dark alcove.

"I wish you would stop reading my mind," she said breathlessly as his hand searched her body in the darkness. His strong hands were caressing her through her tight uniform. She could feel the heat of his body through her suit as his hands cupped her ass.

"Why would you want that?" he whispered against her neck. "If I did not read your mind I would not have been able to see that you want me to do this." His hand slipped around to her front and cupped her pussy through her uniform as he began to rub her. "It is a good thing that I read your mind now and again."

"Oh yes," she whispered against his neck, loving the feeling of him rubbing her, making her want him again. Making the need to fuck him urgent and the foremost important thing in her mind, all she wanted to do was rip off their uniforms and straddle him.

"Commander Kelley, please report to debriefing room number five."

"Dammit," she hissed as T'koh pulled away and stared at the ceiling in wonder, seemingly mesmerized by the computer's voice.

"What was that?"

"A page, I have to answer it." Shana grabbed his hand. "Come on, you better come with me."

She had a bad feeling that this wasn't going to be pretty.

* * * * *

When she got to the debriefing room, she sat T'koh down on a chair and gave him the strictest instructions not to move. Gathering up her courage, she punched in her code and the doors to the debriefing room hissed open.

Stepping across the threshold, she saw that Captain Ventura and Lieutenant Meyers were waiting. Captain Ventura had a grim expression on his face, his eyes red and bloodshot as he sat behind his desk, his hands neatly folded. Lieutenant Meyers wouldn't meet her gaze. He stared over her shoulder, his face pale.

The door slid shut behind her, there was no going back.

"I understand there was a leak in one of the biospheres?"

"Aye, Sir," she said quickly, holding herself at attention.

"Yet, there was no detection of a leak?" Captain Ventura said, cocking an eyebrow. "None of the ensigns assigned to night shift at the biosphere detected any anomalies. Yet, you found something, from your quarters, when your duty shift had ended."

"Aye, Sir. I was on the system, filing my report, and I noticed a leak so minor I felt that I could take care of it myself. I was awake anyway and thought it would be best if I took care of the leak before it got worse."

Captain Ventura grunted. "That is quite admirable of you, Commander Kelley." Captain Ventura stood up and folded his hands behind his back as he paced. "Why would you be on the biosphere's system, Commander? You're in Water Recon, not biosphere habitation."

"With all due respect, Sir, maintaining that biosphere is the only piece of the puzzle we have for restoring water to the Earth's surface. I make it my job to inspect that key, Sir. To make sure our only hope is secured and not at risk of dying or being tampered with by Hazoor insurgents."

Captain Ventura smiled, but Meyers didn't seem happy at all. His eyes were dark like thunderheads as he glared at her.

"At ease, Commander Kelley."

Shana relaxed as Captain Ventura took a seat.

"Captain, I think she should be questioned further," Meyers said urgently. "I've looked at the data, there was no leak, not even a small one."

"Enough, Lieutenant," Captain Ventura said, waving him off. "I trust Commander Kelley's judgment. That's why she's a commander and you're still a lieutenant."

Meyers face went beet red from rage and embarrassment.

"I've been reading your report, Kelley, it seems there is some kind of chasm you've found?"

Shana's eyes flew open as she remembered the passageway her team had found on their mission. Before the electrical storms had started, when she had found T'koh.

"You think there is water down there, Commander?"

"Aye, Sir," she said, as she thought about how mating with T'koh had made the water come. How he had said that mating in the heart would restore the Earth. The passageway that they had found was in the center of the plain, on the horizon was four peaks of ancient mountains. It must be the heart, and if she took T'koh there, she could make the water come. "Permission to take a team down there and explore the cavern as soon as possible, Sir. If there is any water in there, we must reach it before it evaporates."

"Sir, with all due respect, there are serious threats of electrical storms. Sensors showed there was no water in that cavern." Meyers said viciously.

"Yes, and sensors also detected there was no leak, yet there was one. Well, there was something." Captain Ventura glared at Meyers and stood. Leaning over the desk on his knuckles, he stared seriously at her. "We examined the biosphere, we found traces of water," he said it so quietly, whispering it as if he didn't believe it could be true.

"I know, Sir. I think there is water in that cavern, and I think that I will be able to ascertain the means to restore water to the ecosystem."

Captain Ventura smiled and a shiver ran down her spine as they locked eyes across that desk in the debriefing room.

"Take a pod down to the surface."

Chapter Four

"I don't know how I am going to get you on board without being detected," Shana said hurriedly as she gathered what little gear she had to take to the surface.

She had convinced Captain Ventura to allow her to go alone, less chance of contamination. He seemed reluctant at first, but soon acquiesced when she reminded him of all the off-station training she had on the surface. She knew how to survive down there.

Now she was frantically packing a small kit, with T'koh watching her.

"If you take the stone, I shall not be detected or seen. I can make myself unseen if necessary. Do you deem it necessary, Ne-Zhoni?"

A shiver ran down her spine as he said those words. The way he said it, it rolled off his tongue. It made her melt.

"Yes, I do."

T'koh then disappeared, evaporating before her. She dropped her bag and then turned and looked at the stone on her desk, which was glowing a vibrant blue-green. She walked over and picked the stone up, holding it in her palm. It was hot like fire, but it didn't burn, it seemed to pulse with life and energy.

Lie down on your bed, close your eyes.

Shana clenched the stone in her fist and lay down on her bed, taking a deep breath, she closed her eyes. The light in her quarters went out, she opened her eyes and looked around. A gust of wind blew through her room, brushing against her body like a warm caress.

Close your eyes, Ne-Zhoni. Trust me.

Nodding, she rested her head against her pillow and closed her eyes. The sound of rain began to patter against her ceiling and she knew that it wasn't her sound system playing the recording. This felt real.

A light brush of fingers down her body and she felt her uniform being unzipped and tugged off her. The turquoise pulsed in her hand.

You see, I can be undetectable, Ne-Zhoni.

The warm air surrounded her body, her nipples hardened at the brush against them. Her nerves tingling with anticipation, her skin becoming wet with his invisible touch. Moaning, she didn't want it this way, she wanted to see him. She wanted to touch him and taste him.

"Open your eyes, *Ne-Zhoni*."

Looking up, she saw him kneeling between her legs, his cock large and erect, he was naked just as she was.

"I want to taste you," she murmured, setting aside the now cold turquoise on her nightstand. "I want to feel you, I want to fuck you."

T'koh mumbled. "You want to have your way with me?"

"Yes," she growled ferociously. She sat up and grabbed him by the shoulders, pushing him down so that he was lying on the bed. She scraped her nails across his bronze muscular chest, fanning her hair across his skin. "I want to put you through the same torture you put me through."

Straddling his chest so that her ass was in his face, she palmed his cock and brought it to her mouth, tasting the salty musk of his skin. She heard him let out a curse, some muffled plea as he bucked up at her. His strong hands grabbing her waist as his massive cock filled her mouth. She ran her tongue around the head, her other hand began to rhythmically move up and down his base, stroking it as she sucked.

Shana reveled in the feeling of him in her mouth, the taste as she ran her tongue up and down his scrotum, she cried out as she felt his hot hands on her ass, spreading her cheeks as his mouth found her pussy.

T'koh was licking her cunt as he rubbed her clit with the pad of his thumb.

"Oh God," she cried out. Her legs were shaking as she held herself still feeling his mouth against her wet core.

She had never sixty-nined before, but she liked it now. Boy did she ever. She returned her mouth to his cock and began to increase the tempo, scraping her teeth lightly over his erection.

The faster she went, the faster his thumb moved against her clit. T'koh was making it unbearable, she could feel her orgasm building, the tension, the pleasure.

"Fuck," she murmured, pulling away from him. She spun around and straddled his hips, impaling herself hard on his shaft.

"By Creator," he cried out, throwing his head back, she could see his Adam's apple bobbing up and down as he panted. When he looked at her again, his eyes were dark. "*Ne-Zhoni.*"

"I'm going to fuck you so hard." Her voice hitching in her throat as she used her knees to slide off him before slamming back down on him.

T'koh growled and closed his eyes, his hands on her hips. She pulled them away, holding him down by his wrists.

"No way, buddy," she said stilling her movements as he moaned and bucked up against her. "I'm controlling this ride, and I'm going to ride you hard."

Although he was much larger than she, much stronger, he didn't fight her as she leaned over him, pinning him to the mattress. She held him there as she increased her tempo, riding up and down his huge cock. He filled her so completely, he hit all the right places as she rode him with ease.

"*Ne-Zhoni*, please touch yourself," T'koh pleaded. "I want to see you touch yourself."

Letting go of his hands, she sat up and rubbed her breast with one hand and her clit with the other as she grinded against his loins. T'koh bucked up at her and she began to undulate faster, rubbing her clit harder and harder as his hips pounded up to meet her.

"Oh fuck," she cried out. His hands grasped her hips.

"Will you let me, *Ne-Zhoni*?" he was asking her permission to increase the depth of his thrust, to take over her ride.

"Yes," she said breathlessly nodding and she ran her hands through her hair. Pulling out of her, he flipped her on her back. He knelt between her legs and spread her legs wide. Grasping her hips, he thrust into her swiftly, keeping his hold on her hips he held her up, controlling her movements as he fucked her hard. Throwing back her head and closing her eyes, she could feel the fine mist of water touching her skin as he mated with her wildly.

T'koh's thumb rubbed her clit hard, and it wasn't long before she felt that ball of tension begin to expand, like it was ready to explode out of her.

"Oh God, I'm going to come." The muscles in her cunt began to contract and squeeze around his cock. The pleasure washing over her as the mist turned to rain, soaking her body and her hair.

A few more thrusts and T'koh stilled as he came inside her, his hot seed filling her. She thanked modern medicine for the once-a-year shot she took to protect her from anything she could catch or a pregnancy. She wondered what it must have been like in the ancient days on Earth, when they had condoms, how clinical it must of felt, rubber between two lovers.

Opening her eyes, she watched the rain as it dropped onto her bed, but only her bed. It only covered her and T'koh. Panting, he looked down at her as the rain began to stop.

"Never has a mate done that to me."

"What, give you a blowjob?"

"Aye, I knew what it was from your mind, but I had no idea what it would feel like."

"That just seems odd, you know how to give oral sex to a woman, but you have never had a blowjob?"

As the rain stopped, he ran his fingers through his soaking wet hair and looked at her soberly. "It was my job to pleasure the woman, not the other way around."

Shana scooted up so that she was sitting in front of him. "How did you get to be a rain god? Were you born of celestial parents or something?"

T'koh looked at her like she was crazy. "No, I was mortal once."

Hello. "You were a human being once? When?"

"A long time ago, when the Mother Earth was still young and the moon was much larger and brighter in the sky."

"So, how did you get this job?"

"I was cursed by Father Sky," T'koh said stoically, hanging his head in shame. "I was a young, proud, foolish warrior. I killed an eagle to earn my feathers instead of braving a nest to capture one. Father Sky was cross, the eagle was his son. So Mother Earth and Father Sky imprisoned me in the turquoise. I would be the rain god, as their son had once been. I would be called upon in times of drought, to restore balance."

"Forever?" Shana asked quietly. If he was going to disappear after they made the water come, she wasn't sure that she wanted to do that just yet. She found herself not wanting him to go.

"Until I could resurrect Father Sky and Mother Earth, only then would I be free. That time has not come."

Leaning over to him, she touched his cheek and then kissed him lightly. "Perhaps then this is the time of your freedom. Father Sky has not rained down on Mother Earth in centuries. Maybe this is your chance to be free."

* * * * *

Shana stood on the bridge of the small one-person pod. She controlled the flight as they broke into orbit around the Earth, flying the small vessel so that it lined up with the Great Plains continent where she had been doing her recon. The cavern that they had found was marked with a beacon, so she knew where she would have to land.

T'koh stood beside her and watched the view screen in wonder as they flew toward the brown arid surface of Mother Earth.

She had managed to sneak him on the pod undetected. The turquoise was in the small pouch attached to her off-station uniform.

"Such wonders," T'koh whispered. "To see Mother Earth as Father Sky would, she is beautiful…even in death."

Shana nodded. "So what happens if say the curse were broken? What happens to you?"

"I cease to exist. Or so the legend says."

Swallowing hard, Shana cleared her throat. "Is that what you want? I mean, we could just go about our business and try to restore water another way. We don't have to mate in the heart."

Shana felt a hand slip around her waist. "I must, *Ne-Zhoni*. As much as I long to stay with you, I must do this unselfish thing, to rectify my wrongs and the selfish act I committed when I killed that eagle. I have to do this, and I hope that you will assist me."

Shana kept the tears that threatened to spill from her eyes at bay. She nodded and cleared her throat once more. "Of course, yes. I will do this to help you."

T'koh took her hand and brushed a kiss off her knuckles. "Thank you."

Shana nodded and stared out of the view screen, watching as the brown parched Earth loomed up before her, blacking out the space that surrounded them.

"I think you should turn this pod around." A click sound and a high-pitched whistle of a laser charging caused them both to turn around.

Shana saw Lieutenant Meyers standing behind them, a blaster pointed straight at them.

"Don't move, Commander Kelley. I have this blaster charged at vaporize."

"What are you doing, Lieutenant?" she asked keeping her wits about her. Meyers was nervous and edgy. She had never seen him like this before.

"I'm telling you to turn this pod around. You have something planned to restore water to the Earth and I want to know what it is."

"Why? So you can take credit for it."

"No," Meyers said, taking a step closer. "Because whatever it is, I aim to stop you."

T'koh growled and stepped forward, but Shana held him at bay.

"Why would you want to stop me? We're both high-ranking officers of Water Recon, it's our goal to restore water to the planet."

Meyers laughed. "Why would I want that? I'm head of the Hazoor faction. Earth is dead and your team is obsolete."

"You?"

"Yes, did you think it was some sort of vagrant? I founded the Hazoor faction when I was at the Academy. The more I studied Earth, the more I realized that it was a useless endeavor to try to restore it. Especially, when we can mimic the appropriate biospheres in space."

"Yet man is not meant for Father Sky," T'koh said, moving toward Meyers. Meyers swung his blaster at him, surprised by T'koh's sudden presence.

"Who the fuck are you?" Meyers screamed.

"That does not matter, put down the weapon." T'koh said seriously, taking another step forward.

"Keep away from me," Meyers warned, shaking the blaster. "Or I'll vaporize you into atoms."

Shana took her opportunity to back slowly to the warning alarm. Pressing the button, she typed in the simple message. The numerical code that would dispatch the security team, letting them know that her pod was under a terrorist attack from Hazoor insurgents.

"What are you doing? You bitch!" Meyers hand dug into her shoulder and he spun her around, slapping her hard with the back of his hand, it split her lip and she fell to the floor.

"You do not touch Shana that way," T'koh growled.

Meyers turned around and fired the laser blaster at T'koh. Shana screamed as she watched in horror. When the smoke cleared she let out a sob of joy when she saw T'koh standing there, unaffected.

"What the fuck?" Meyers cursed, looking at his blaster.

"You cannot harm me with your weapons of light." T'koh said matter-of-factly. Meyers had no time to react as T'koh grabbed him and threw him against the wall of the pod. Meyer's blaster slid across the floor with a clatter and Shana grabbed it.

Standing to her feet, she held the gun on Meyers. He looked up at her. "I think your faction days are over." Pushing a button, she secured Meyers behind a portable force field.

A warning buzzer went off and she looked over her shoulder to see that the pod was careening out of control toward one the mountains.

"Oh my God."

T'koh took the blaster from her. "Go, I shall watch this cretin who wishes harm to mankind."

Nodding, Shana handed the blaster to T'koh and focused on leveling the flight of the pod.

"Commander Kelley, we received your distress call."

"Aye," Shana said, smoothing out the pod and bringing it to rest on the planet's surface, by the heart. "The leader of the Hazoor faction attacked us on the pod. We've got him secured."

"We're sending a security detachment to the planet's surface. We should be there within the hour, but what do you mean 'we', Commander? There is no clearance on that pod for another individual."

"I meant me, sorry. Commander Kelley, over and out."

Switching the communicator off, she turned to see T'koh staring in wonder at the force field that kept Meyers trapped.

"Will he be of no threat here?"

"Right, in about twenty seconds he will no longer be a threat." Shana pushed another button and gas filtered in the confined space that held Meyers.

"What did you do?" T'koh asked as Meyers head drooped to his shoulder.

"Sleeping gas, no one should interrupt us now."

T'koh nodded. "Then let us go, bring back order to the Earth."

* * * * *

T'koh had refused the heavier suit to protect him from the harshness of Earth's environment. Shana didn't push it. If the man could survive a laser blast set to vaporization then he could survive the quick jaunt to the cavern from the pod.

As they stepped outside, Shana could see an approaching electrical storm, one like she had never seen, moving fast across the gray sky.

T'koh raised his head and opened his arms. "Father Sky knows I am here and what I am to do." He took her gloved hand. "What we are to do."

Shana swallowed hard at the thought of mating with him in the cavern deep below the Earth's surface. The thought of restoring the ecosystem was a heady proposition. *What will it be like to live on Earth again?* Would she get planet sickness? Would the animals and the plants adapt again to the place their ancestors once grew?

She remembered the time she had visited the Great Atlantic Valley, a large crack in the Earth that seemed to go on forever in some places, all the caverns, mountains and valleys that stretched for miles and miles. She learned in school that the valley used to be filled to the brim with water. Water that covered two-thirds of the Earth's surface and contained abundant life, like fish and whales. *What did they look like?* They had the sufficient DNA to breed fish and whales, but they were unable to sustain them and study them on the space station.

Shana looked up at T'koh as he led her to the covered opening and she felt a shiver ran down her spine. She shouldn't really put all her hopes in this man, this rain god, but she couldn't help it.

T'koh pulled back the cover of the little domed hut that protected the chasm's opening. Shana switched on the torchlight that was imbedded into her wrist strap and they stepped inside the stifling hut.

"You can take off that heavy suit, *Ne-Zhoni*. It is not made from the Earth and will insult our mother." T'koh began to strip off his clothes.

"I can't, the radiation—"

"Nothing will touch you now, *Ne-Zhoni*. The only thing that will touch you in the heart is me."

Her blood fired and she began to peel off her bio suit until she was almost naked. All that she wore was a tight pair of briefs and an Interstellar issue sports bra. T'koh was completely naked and her body reacted to the sight of his magnificent form in the shadows of the domed hut. Even when he wasn't aroused he was still an impressive sight.

A breeze suddenly whipped up from the crack in the Earth. A cool air licked at her hot sultry skin, she shivered and crossed her arms tightly around her chest.

"What was that?"

"The heart," T'koh said, taking her hand. "Come."

They didn't need a torchlight, the cavern seemed to be glowing and as they descended down the rough-hewn stairwell. She stared in wonder at the layers of mineral and rock as they descended. Glittering minerals and gems cemented into the walls, like she had never seen before.

"Beautiful," she whispered to herself. She let her fingers trail across the surface of the rock, feeling it seemingly pulse under her fingers.

"Mother Earth is not dead." T'koh chuckled to himself. "She lives still, she is just asleep."

Gooseflesh broke across her skin as they descended deeper and deeper into the cavern. Then she heard it, the sound of a drip and rushing that seemed to grow louder as they traveled closer to the heart.

It can't be. Shaking her head, she tried to still her heart. She didn't want to be disappointed by a possible figment of her imagination.

"Is that..."she trailed off as the rushing sound grew louder and louder.

"It is," T'koh said, turning to face her in the darkness. "Water—Mother Earth knows that I am here."

T'koh stopped and touched a wall, the small chamber deep in the Earth seemed to light up and glow an iridescent blue.

Rain God

"Oh my God," Shana whispered, squinting as she looked around. The walls of the little subterranean cave were covered in turquoise. The blue-green glistening and reverberating made her curious to see what the turquoise was reflecting. Water, lots of clear, cold water.

Panting, she knelt down and touched the pool of water. She had never seen water so clear, so deep before. It was like a lake.

"What do you think of the heart, *Ne-Zhoni*?"

"I don't how this is possible," she said, standing up staring at the glowing blue cave in wonder. "Our sensors should've been able to pick it up."

"No," T'koh said, shaking his head. "Like me, this water only shows itself when it wants to be seen, and it wants to be seen by you." He let go of her hand and took a step into the water. She jumped back as the water came up above his waist, he held out a wet arm to her. "Come, we must swim to the center to complete our quest."

"You're contaminating it," she shrieked hysterically. "Section fifteen of the Water Recon Act—"

"I am not harming the water. Come, *Ne-Zhoni*, do not be afraid."

Shana's body was shaking as she nodded her head. She peeled off her bra and her underwear and left them on the rough-hewn stairs. Taking his wet, cool hand, she stepped into the water. The waves lapped at her toes and she laughed nervously, a sob catching in her throat at the feeling of the water surrounding her, enveloping her.

Sinking down in the pool, she was amazed at how light her body felt. Her feet touched the smooth bottom of turquoise and then she saw a flash of silver.

"What was that?" she cried, jumping up in T'koh's arms.

"Have you never seen a fish before?" he asked, chuckling.

"A fish?" She pushed out of his arms and watched in wonder as the small school of tiny fish flickered against the glowing turquoise wall, swimming past her toes and tickling her before zooming off out of the glowing cave toward the darkness.

"A school of fish, I believe. My last incarnation there was an interesting book by a man named Darwin. One of the white men had it." T'koh ducked under the water and as he resurfaced the water droplets clung to him, sparkling on his skin.

Shana giggled and then immersed herself. The water went up her nose. She hadn't been prepared for that. She resurfaced coughing, water covering her so completely. It cooled her, relaxed her.

T'koh was laughing. "I take it by your reaction that you probably have never swum before."

Rubbing the water from her eyes, she swallowed some. "Right."

He swam up beside her, she could feel his body heat through the water and then felt him pressed against her. "Hold on to my neck and do not let go."

Shana wrapped her arms around him and T'koh began to glide through the water. She cried out and held tighter, but soon relaxed at the feel of breaking across the water's surface so smoothly. She reveled in the feel of T'koh's tight buttocks bouncing against her stomach as he glided through the water, the water rushing over her body as T'koh swam. It excited her. This moment, the moment of discovery, was the most erotic moment of her life.

"You can stand here, *Ne-Zhoni*."

Shana let go of his neck and put her feet down on the cool turquoise bottom of the clear crystal pool. Standing in the water, she watched as T'koh pulled himself out of the crystal pool and onto the small turquoise island in the center of the lake, the water slid off his body in diamond droplets and she held her breath as she watched. He turned and held out his hand, she grasped it and he pulled her up so that she stood in front of him, her wet naked body pressed against his. She could feel his cock hardening against her belly.

"So this is it, the heart?" she asked, staring up into his dark eyes.

"Yes," he said, brushing her lips with his. Closing her eyes, she felt his hands slide through her soaking wet hair. "Your tresses are like silk, *Ne-Zhoni*."

T'koh kissed her and she opened her mouth to his tongue. Shana tested him deeply as his hand slid from her hair down her back to cup her ass and bring her flush against his loins. He squeezed the cheeks of her bottom, kneading them as his tongue intertwined with hers.

Shana pulled away and began to kiss his neck and his chest, inching herself lower, eager to take his large cock in her mouth. T'koh stopped her and pulled her up.

"No, I am not to receive pleasure with your touch. Only I can pleasure you, that is the only way to make the rain come."

Moaning, she nodded as he knelt down, his hands circling her waist pulling her cunt to his lips. Snaking her fingers through his hair, she shuddered in pleasure as his hot tongue parted her folds to lick her clit, darting quickly up and down. Two of his fingers entered her, gently pumping in and out of her in the same rhythm as his tongue.

"Oh God, please fuck me," she cried out as she felt the heat of an orgasm unfurling in her belly. Before she knew what was happening, he slid his fingers out and laid her down on the cool turquoise floor. She was so wet, she wanted him so badly.

T'koh spread her legs wide and thrust into her, crying out her name as his big cock buried in her pussy to the hilt. She bucked her hips, urging him to fuck her senseless.

Shana wasn't disappointed as he began to pump in and out of her wildly. T'koh thrust into her hard, her hips meeting his. He braced his weight on one arm as his free hand rubbed her clit in time with his hips.

Her breasts bounced up and down as and she threw her head back running her fingers through her damp hair. She could feel her muscles contracting, the pleasure building inside her as they mated in the heart. Shana reached out and her fingers touched water, the lake rising around them.

"*Ne-Zhoni*, please come with me," T'koh said through gritted teeth. His body taut, like a bowstring. She didn't make him wait too long as the wave of pleasure washed through her, her pussy clamping down on his cock, milking him as she came.

T'koh shouted and stilled as he came inside her. Then she heard it, the sound of rumbling above them. Not like any thunder she had ever heard before. There was a roaring surrounding her.

Shana opened her eyes and saw that the lake was getting deeper, filling the cavern. T'koh slid out of her and scooped her up in his arms. He quickly sank into the water and she held tight to his neck as he quickly swam back toward the stone-cut stairs.

When they reached the side she clambered off him and grabbed her bra and underwear. She quickly dressed as he pulled himself out of the lake.

"What's happening?" she asked with a hint of panic in her voice.

"Mother Earth is waking up," there was another roar of thunder rumbling above them and T'koh smiled at her, rubbing his thumb across her cheek. "And Father Sky is quite happy to meet her again. Quickly, to the surface before this whole cavern fills."

Nodding, she ran up the stairs two at a time with T'koh on her heels. Breaking through the surface, she ran out of the stifling hut and stood outside.

"Oh my God," she whispered as pitch-black thunderheads rolled in from all directions. The wind whipped

Rain God

around her, and the air was heavy and still. She had never seen anything like it.

As she stood there with T'koh she heard him laugh out loud.

"What?" she asked, turning toward him. He was bent over, his hands on his knees. T'koh stood up straight and his eyes were shining as he held up his palms, bloody. "Oh my God, what happened?"

"Nothing, don't you see?" he said, staring at the blood on his skin. "My knees are cut."

Shana laughed. "I'm not surprised, you were using them quite vigorously down there, the ground was made of turquoise."

"No, I mean...that is not what I mean. The curse is broken, I have not bled in thousands of years. I have not bled since that day I killed the eagle."

"Does that mean you stay here...with me?"

"Aye, if you'll let me, Shana," T'koh said, stepping toward her.

Her heart was beating wildly against her chest. T'koh was free from the turquoise, free from his curse. She had been so afraid that he would disappear after the ceremony or die, it never occurred to her that he would live and stay with her.

Opening her mouth, she meant to answer, but five pods landed, surrounding them. A security detachment led by Captain Ventura poured out the pods, all their blasters trained on T'koh.

"Commander Kelley, is this the Hazoor insurgent?"

"No," Shana said, stepping between T'koh and the blasters. "No, Lieutenant Meyers was the secret insurgent, and in fact he is the leader of the faction. I have him detained in my pod." She pointed.

Captain Ventura nodded and security began to run toward her shuttle.

"And what of the water?" he asked, eyeing a very naked T'koh. A flush of embarrassment crept up her cheeks at her own undressed state. Captain Ventura motioned and two blankets were produced by a security official. She quickly covered herself and T'koh wrapped the blanket around his waist, seemingly unaffected by his nudity.

"Well, Sir—"

The thunder boomed above them and Captain Ventura craned his neck toward the sky. Then it happened, a drop fell from the low clouds to the parched earth at her feet. Between Captain Ventura and herself.

Ventura looked down at the ground stunned, his face went pale as he stared at the droplet of rain that soaked into the ground. Shana bent down and touched the wet dirt, feeling the soft sand under her fingertips.

Then the thunder rolled again and the sky opened up on them. Water began to pour out of the sky and bubble up from the cracks in the Earth.

Shana smiled as Captain Ventura's lips trembled. The security officers around her began to peel off their protective shielding. They removed their helmets and stared up into the sky as the rain poured down on them in a torrent.

"Well, I'll be dammed." Captain Ventura said peeling off his helmet and letting the rain wash over him. He let out a whoop of joy and punched his fist toward the sky. Shana laughed and jumped up and down. Turning around, she saw T'koh standing there, his smile bright, his arms held open.

Running, she flung herself in his arms and he spun her around, kissing her.

"Yes," she said breathlessly as he put her back on the muddy ground.

"What is yes, *Ne-Zhoni*?"

"Yes, I want you to stay with me. Always."

A smile broke across his face and he kissed her passionately, holding her close.

Epilogue
One year later

🙞

Shana stood on what used to be the edge of The Great Atlantic Valley. She stared out over a vast ocean. She never got tired of hearing the surf and the waves crash against the shore, watching the waves break in the distant against the horizon.

Shana looked all around her, the Earth had changed a lot in the last year. It was no longer brown and dead, green was sprouting up from the soil. The cry of a gull filled the air. She looked up to see it swooping and gliding across the blue sky. She had been promoted after the rain had come, and the rain came frequently. The ancient weather detecting equipment was being upgraded to track rain and she was now in charge of seeding and restocking the planet, with T'koh's help of course.

A smile tugged at her lips as she watched the lone sea gull fly off. She never dreamed that she would be standing here, watching the Earth come to life again. In twenty years the ecosystem would be stable enough to sustain man again. Well, for those who wished to return to the Earth's surface.

The Hazoor faction had completely fallen apart with Meyer's incarceration. Nothing was stopping them from returning Earth to her former glory.

"There you are, Captain Kelley."

Turning, she saw T'koh in a pair of cotton pants and bare chested, he walked from their hut out on to the beach.

"Yes, Commander T'koh, how can I help you?"

"I have my report, Commander," he said, a sly smile tugging at the corner of his lips. He wrapped his hands around her waist and pulled her close.

"Well, it's about time. I don't like any of my seeding officers to be late with their reports. I have to punish them if they don't file them on time."

T'koh leaned his forehead against her and smiled, running his fingers through her hair.

"Oh? And how will you punish your one and only officer in this sector?"

Laughing, she pushed him down on the sand, unbuttoning her cotton blouse. "Oh I'll show you, Rain God, I'll show you."

The End

FERAL MOON
Regina Carlysle

ఴ

Dedication

To Anny Cook, Zen queen and creative genius. Thanks for nudging me in a different direction.

Chapter One

He scented her the moment he entered the smoky club.

His prey. His future.

Amid the smell of humans and sweat, Titus focused his razor-sharp gaze toward the center of the throng and spotted her sitting with a friend. Beneath the muted blue ceiling lights that swept the room, her hair glistened black and shiny hanging just below her shoulder blades. She still wore the simple white blouse and beige skirt she'd worn today at work.

"Shall I keep a lookout, my lord?"

Titus glanced at his first lieutenant and nodded. Diego Luna was here in the city looking for her. It was left to him to take her, mate with her tonight before they found her and all was lost. "Stake out the front of the club," he murmured. "Send Rico and John to watch the back. Be alert."

"Yes, lord."

Titus Declan went further into the room and the crowd seemed to part as if he'd willed it. Of course, he had. As alpha of the southwestern panther tribe, he exuded a presence that commanded respect. Living among the humans for several hundred years, he'd learned to fit in, learned their ways. Were-panthers were solitary creatures during the hunt but their human sides allowed them to live together and thrive. In all these years of rule, times were few that anyone from the Turquoise Moon panther tribe had been seen in their panther form but those humans had either been quickly dispatched or used to serve his purpose.

Such had been the case with Natalie Jones, a human who'd taken the future of their race to raise, after the infant girl's parents had been brutally murdered by the Los Locos

Mexican tribe. They'd been after the child, of course, because she'd been born with psychic powers of prophecy that were without parallel. Titus, himself, had placed the baby girl into the human's arms knowing full well, he would watch over her through her growing years. When she reached her growth and became a woman finally realizing the powers she kept locked deep inside, she would belong to him as his mate.

It was his destiny. And hers.

He felt the large, beautifully worked silver and turquoise ring on his finger heat, sending out energy, calling to him and to her. The turquoise stone was a sign of royalty to his people. His mate wore it as well. Mahara had been given an exact replica on her thirteenth birthday and he knew the stone she wore would be hot to the touch as her body readied itself for his taking. She would be confused. Even now, she seemed a little lost. Titus found an empty table a good distance away and watched her. The lighting in the place was dim but his excellent vision allowed him to consider her. She was coming into her time. He could smell the pheromones, the musk of her, calling to him on the basest level and his cock pulsed, hard and strong in response. His blood heated as it roared through his veins. Power. He felt it simmering inside him. Yes, she was ready for fucking, for taking and he felt sorry about the confusion she must feel right now. All of their women went through the change but for Mahara Jones it would be doubly difficult considering she would also attain her psychic abilities.

"Can I get you a drink?" The waitress sidled up and Titus felt her regard, her lust but he wasn't interested in the human.

"No. Maybe later."

She left on a cloud of heavy perfume and Titus returned to his study of the beautiful Mahara. She'd grown into a lovely, caring woman and much of that was due to the human Natalie. He'd personally seen to it her life had been one of quality and privilege, paid for her education and eventually hired her as personnel director for Declan Technologies. She only knew him as her employer and as the company was a huge sprawling empire, they had little contact but the most casual. That had been of utmost importance. Diego Luna had searched for her for years and it had been important to maintain a certain distance.

That distance would come to an end tonight.

Spies were everywhere and there was no doubt every male were-panther in the area knew a female was coming into her time.

Tonight he would take her, fuck her, make Mahara his. The binding ritual would be done. Soon. And Diego Luna could go to hell.

Mahara Jones looked into the brilliant green depths of the appletini that sat on the table in front of her and tried for all she was worth to look normal. She wasn't and she knew it. It took an enormous effort to appear as if she fitted in tonight. Harder than it had ever been before. Shaking off the uncomfortable sensation that whipped up her spine and zipped impatient fingers over every inch of her scalp, she sent her gaze skimming around the darkened club and zeroed in on the gyrating couples on the dance floor. Rock music blasted through the room setting her every last nerve on edge.

It was as if she could feel every note shimmer across her skin.

She fought the urge to run her hands through her hair. It felt as if a million ants marched across her flesh. Foreboding thrummed a steady beat through her brain but she fought it off and faced her friend who was treating her to a birthday drink before she headed home.

"You seem off tonight, hon." Trish propped her elbows on the table, giving her a speculative look. "Drink up. God, you're so uptight tonight. You have been all day. Hell, all week. What's wrong? I swear a dozen guys have asked you to dance but you turn them all down."

"Maybe I don't feel like celebrating. I should be with Mom tonight. It was just the two of us for so long and I guess I just feel discombobulated."

Trish reached across the highly polished table and took her hand. "You miss her so much, don't you?"

Sudden tears burned behind her eyes as she thought of her mother's recent death and recalled the haunting words she'd spoken at the moment of her passing. They ran through Mahara's mind like a sinister riddle to which she had no answer.

"What is it?" Trisha pressed. "Tell me."

It is time. Search out your destiny. It is time, my darling, search out your destiny.

Your destiny. Your destiny.

Natalie Jones' words whirled through her mind. Confused. God, she was so confused. Feeling restless, unable to bear Trish's touch on her skin, she drew back her hand and pulled the dark-framed glasses from her face. She propped her elbow on the table and settled her forehead in her hand. Her head throbbed. "You'll think this is nuts."

"Never. Come on. Spill it."

"I was adopted," she blurted, looking up.

Trish's expressive brown eyes widened. "What the hell! She never told you? You're twenty-five years old. She'd have had a million opportunities. Why did she wait so long?"

Mahara shook her head, feeling confused and overly sensitive. Overheated almost. Nerves! It had to be nerves but it was as if just the motion of shaking her head caused her hair to feel ultra heavy. She wore her hair long—to just past her shoulders—and she swore she could identify each strand. Something was going on with her and it scared her to death. "I don't know why she waited. But once she said it, I knew she was right. We were always so different. We looked nothing alike."

"She was fair. Blonde. Come to think of it, there was no resemblance at all."

Sinister feelings swept her and she felt trapped, almost as if she was being hunted. Her mind was muzzy like tiny spiders were busily spinning webs and it had been like this for days. She needed air. She had to get out of here but the idea of standing up made her want to vomit. Sick. Yeah, that was it. She was coming down with the flu.

Eyeing the beautiful turquoise ring she had worn since her thirteenth birthday, she reached out to find the stone was smoldering hot. Again. As hot as fire but yet it didn't hurt to touch it. Impulsively, she reached across the table and laid her hand flat on the surface. She had to know. Was she losing her mind? "Do something for me. Touch my ring."

Trish gave her a quizzical look but quickly reached out to run her finger over the highly polished stone. It was a gorgeous thing and her mother had told her it was very old when she'd presented it to her all those years ago. Set in heavily worked silver that featured the etching of a full moon on either side, the turquoise in the center caught the gleam of low lights and bounced them back.

Trish touched the ring and frowned. "Um. What am I looking for here?"

"It doesn't feel hot to you?"

She shook her head, frowning. "Is it supposed to feel hot? Feels cold to me. Really cold."

Mahara withdrew her hand, more confused than ever. She'd always suspected there was something wrong with her and now she knew. Without warning something came to her. Just a flicker in her mind. Her mouth formed around the name *James* but before she could make a sound, Trish's boyfriend, James, came up behind Trish and planted a noisy kiss on the side of her neck.

Shock whipped through her system and she was so stunned she could only nod mutely when James swept Trish off to the dance floor. Something unexplainable was happening to her and it had been going on for days. It had begun as little things that she'd thought were just weird premonitions. Like James coming up behind Trish when he had. She'd *seen* it in her mind before it happened. And her body. Something bizarre was going on. Every beat of the music made her blood heat and the very core of her body pulse to a pagan tempo. Restlessly, she squirmed in her chair and sent her gaze wildly around the room. Her panties were drenched. Mahara rubbed her thighs together hoping against hope to stem the rising tide. Sexual excitement rose up like a great beast to center in her pussy, deep and pulsing, a release longing to break free. She wanted to grab the nearest man and throw him to the floor and take him like an animal.

Every tiny hair on the back of her neck rose to attention and Mahara's heart thumped sharply in her chest. The turquoise stone in her ring heated against the finger on her right hand where she wore it. Lifting her glasses, she settled them back on her nose but she didn't need them any longer and wearing them was just stupid. A visit to her eye doctor would only tell her what she already knew. Her vision seemed to have perfected itself overnight. Impossible. Through the lenses, the ring went fuzzy. Mahara huffed a breath and yanked them off, shoved them in her purse just as their waitress came up. "Drink?"

"Um, no. But could you do me a favor?"

"Sure."

Mahara glanced toward the dance floor. "Could you tell my friend that I have to take off?"

"No problem."

Shakily, she got to her feet and slung the strap of her purse over her shoulder intending to walk the few blocks to her downtown apartment. The feeling of being stalked hit her in a giant wave and she felt her knees start to buckle but she caught herself on the edge of the table. Suddenly, a huge hand wrapped around her elbow to steady her and she looked up to see her boss, the great Titus Declan staring down at her.

She'd never seen or known a more devastating man. Big, brawny, ripped with muscle, he looked like a Viking bent on plunder with that longer-than-fashionable black hair and weird golden eyes. But he was her boss. She barely knew him. Suddenly, she blinked. "Mr. Declan."

"Titus."

"Um. Hi."

"Let me help you."

Mahara felt her legs turn to rubber. The warmth of his touch seeped through the cotton of her blouse and a wave of longing, of heat swept her. The ring seemed to vibrate against her hand. Wetness, created by an awful lust, drenched her, seeped from her core. She wanted sex. Craved it. Oh God! She was in big trouble and didn't know what to do about it. Tears filled her eyes as she stared up at him. "Help me."

"Come on."

Without another word, he put his arm around her and drew her close to his body. She had the sudden insane urge to sink into him and crawl up the all that brawn and take his mouth. She wanted his cock soothing the awful ache in her pussy. His smell was intoxicating. Mahara felt her heart thump wildly in her chest. "I-I think someone put something in my drink," she managed.

He only tightened his grip. His hand skimmed her arm and a shiver followed in its wake. Sweat beaded her forehead. When they reached the entrance to the club, he drew her to the brick wall near the front door. Neon white from the overhead sign splashed light intermittently over his feral features. The front of his shirt grazed her nipples and she gasped at the feel of the firm muscles beneath the fabric. Pleasure-pain, wicked sensation, made her moan.

"Shh."

"What's wrong with me?" Mahara gripped his sides and stared up at him. "I'm so embarrassed."

"Don't be. All will be clear soon."

"I don't understand."

He pressed his lips to her forehead as he replied. "Soon. You'll understand soon."

This man was her boss. She barely knew him except for lusting after him from afar. All the women did. It was practically an office sport. Now he was here, rescuing her, pressing his big body against hers as if he had every right to do so.

A group of laughing people approached the club and Titus wasted no time in getting her away. He put his arm around her and drew her into a dark alcove near the side of the business. A partial wall, shrubs and trees hid the tiny spot from view leaving it totally dark. As the chatter and laughter faded, the only sounds were from traffic on the nearest street. Once again, she found herself pressed to a wall. Aside from that single element, it felt they were completely isolated from the outside world. An air of intimacy surrounded them. Mahara noted his breathing seemed to match her own. Quick and sharp.

Titus looked at her, then glanced over his shoulder.

"Kevin?"

"Yes, lord." Another man's voice came from the other side of the wall.

"Bring my car around to the curb at the north side of the building. Stay with it until I get there."

Mahara once again felt his full attention and she trembled beneath that harsh golden gaze. His muscles shifted beneath her hands. "Are you all right?"

She shook her head. "N-no. Something is happening to me and I don't know what it is. Everything feels crazy and upside down like I have no control over anything."

"You don't." His voice was harsh, grim. He muttered a low curse. "Better let me take the edge off then I'll take you home."

Before she could absorb his words, he reached for the buttons on her blouse.

"What are y—"

"Shh, Mahara, you must trust me."

The touch of his hands brushing against her breasts, stole every last breath from her lungs and a fine sweat broke over her from top to toe. As if from a distance, she felt the front snap of her bra give way and suddenly her breasts were held firmly in his warm hands. Mahara gasped. A moan soon followed as he swept his thumbs over her hard, aching nipples. "Titus."

And then his mouth took hers in the hottest kiss this side of hell, that tender burning on her breasts nothing when compared to the flames that whipped up wild and fierce through her belly. His tongue dipped, sank deep to drink in a thorough tasting that made her arch against him. Her pussy throbbed in response. Nothing at that moment was more important than getting him inside her. While his fingers plucked and pulled at her nipples she made a whimpering sound.

"You're delicious," he breathed against her neck. "Feel me. Feel how hard my cock has become at the simple thought of burying it deep inside you."

Frantic need whipped up and caught her. Lifting her leg to his hip, she brought him close and felt the truth of his words. Raking against the rigid length hidden from her by the fine wool of his slacks, she repeated the motion slowly, then quicker, quicker, speed and the need blasting through her channel, made her helpless.

Titus made a strange coughing sound, a sort of slow growl and latched onto a bare nipple to suck hard. A sharp longing stabbed deep inside her as he took her hips and pressed her hard against the brick wall at her back. Sensation grabbed and twisted with each pull of his mouth, each rasping of his cock against her sopping wet cunt. The ball of pleasure and tension tightened unbearably until she begged for completion. She was frantic for it. Then he pivoted his hips, caught her clit on a strong pass and that ever-tightening ball inside her blew apart as if detonated by explosives.

A scream rose up, high and sharp from her throat but he covered her mouth and drank the sound, swallowing it whole while she could do nothing but tremble.

His arms went around her and she sank against him breathing hard and the feeling she experienced was tremendous but the relief was short lived. Without warning, heat flashed through her belly again. Stronger than before. "No," she breathed. "Oh no."

Titus drew back, cupped her face and leaned close enough she could feel his warm breath caress her face. "I will take care of you, Mahara. You must trust me."

Chapter Two
∞

After he hauled her beautiful ass into the far backseat of the limo and the vehicle pulled away from the curb, he drew her up into his lap. Gods! He ached. His erection was so large, his balls so tight, he thought he'd explode if he didn't get inside her sweetness soon. Normally he didn't travel so ostentatiously but after feeling the turquoise stone begin to heat early this morning and then catching her scent when she passed his office this afternoon, he'd asked his first lieutenant to fetch the limo.

More privacy for what was to come.

She was a beautiful female, with her wealth of black hair, sapphire eyes and lush curves. He would explore each hill and valley before he was through but he already knew he'd never get enough of her. The rich female scent of her instantly filled the backseat of the limo and he had to have her.

Titus gathered her close. She was whimpering now, in the throes of the powerful lust that took their women when their maturing time came. Gritting his teeth, he pulled her across his lap. He yanked up the modest, straight skirt she wore and, ignoring his own raging need, shoved his hand into the front of her soaked panties.

"Blessed gods! You feel like wet silk against my fingers." He stroked the smooth flesh of her mons. Like all women of his species, she had no body hair. Delicious. He could barely wait to taste her fully, to part the petals of her sex with his tongue and drink the juices that flowed like honey from her body. In all his years, he'd never wanted a female more. "Sweet. Smooth. I love the feel of you."

When Mahara buried her face against his neck, a fierce, possessive urgency caught him up. The gums over his fangs tingled in expectation of the claiming to come. Wanting nothing interfering with his pleasure and hers, he ripped her tiny panties from her legs. Her sensible pumps hit the floor of the limo with a couple of muted thumps. Titus touched and teased her flesh, tweaked the lips of her sex, then sent his fingers deep into her sweet cunt. His possession of her had already begun in a small way but soon, yes, soon, she would be completely his. The pleasure of it, the sense of completion he felt was beyond anything he'd experienced over all the centuries of his life. Together they would rule their panther tribe, their powerful army of shifters with strength and compassion. With the additional benefit of the hybrid psychic powers passed to her by her mother, she would be the perfect mate.

Mahara began to writhe in his arms, her ass rubbing with devastating precision against his cock, making Titus catch his breath. With a low, aching sound, she leaned even closer and sank her teeth against his neck, flicking with her tongue, driving him crazy. His response was to find her swollen clit with unerring accuracy. Pinching the bundle of nerves, teasing slowly, then quicker, he continued to play when suddenly she stiffened. Due to the soundproof nature of the limo, he let her wail as she fell apart. With his fingers buried in her drenched heat so deeply, he felt every shiver, every contraction and the knowledge those very same muscles would soon milk him to completion filled him with a fierce urgency to take her now.

But no.

Not yet.

He tightened his hold on her, loving that he finally had the right to touch her this way. He'd dreamed of it for years. After tonight too, she would be safe from the predatory tribes that were scattered across America, Mexico and Canada. Diego Luna could take his soldiers and go home. It was done. Or at least it would be once he'd marked her and taken her as his mate. Once that was done their inbred code of honor would take hold and they would return to their homeland.

"Where are we going?" she whispered against his throat. She was completely relaxed despite the fact her body still twitched slightly. His heart tightened, emotion rising quickly, emotion that he'd felt little of over the past years. He kept his hand over her mound offering intimate comfort as he gentled her. "I know you're not taking me home because you don't know where I live."

"I know everything about you, sweet one." Titus buried his nose in her fragrant hair and just breathed her in. "Shh, now. Be still. You need to rest while you can. We're going to my compound."

"Um. That sounds ominous."

He laughed. His first laugh in years. Had his life been that hollow? Yes, he quickly realized. It had. "Not scary at all. It's beautiful. I think you'll like it."

"You think?"

He kissed the top of her head. "I know."

Finally he reached out and pressed the speaker button that was set in the door. "How long, Kevin?"

"Not much longer, lord. Probably another five minutes."

Titus depressed the button and saw Mahara watching him warily. "Lord?" Then a tiny smile appeared on her face. "That's taking the employer-employee relationship a bit far, don'cha think?" Then she laughed, the sound thrilling him. "You're *my* boss. Do you expect me to call you *lord*?"

He scoffed at that and shook his head. "Hardly. You, my lovely, are an equal in every way."

"Mm. I'm glad you think so." Then, as trusting as a child, she rested against him and for just a minute he forgot his cock ached like a son of a bitch. *Later*, he reminded himself, *best to go gently. For now.*

By the time, the limo pulled up at the front gate, Mahara was sleeping. Having kept up with her progress in school and later college, he knew she had a bright, curious mind so he knew it was a testament to her complete exhaustion that she could doze considering tonight's events. When he was done with her tonight, she would no doubt want to sleep for a week. *Let her enjoy the respite*, he thought, as Kevin drove the limo through the electronic gate and to the front of the house.

In the time it took to stop the car, Mahara began to shake and tremble in his arms. A heavy moan broke from her full pink lips. She was nearing another crisis. He could feel it in the way heat rolled from the surface of her skin, by the flush that rose on her cheeks. There was no time to lose. He stroked his hand slowly over her throat, her shoulder and down the length of her arm. His fingers brushed across the surface of the perfect turquoise stone she wore and felt it pulse as if alive. The rich scent of her body preparing itself for him filled the small space.

Her eyes snapped open, a wild look flickered there. "You should take me to the hospital. Now." The pitch of her voice rose and he felt her terror. "Maybe they can pump my stomach. Make it stop. Titus!"

His heart squeezed tightly. Tonight he would rock her world in more ways than one but he would stay with her every moment until the truth of things settled in. "A hospital can't help you, Mahara. Only I can. You must trust me."

Another sharp sound came from her. Her body jerked as if it had been struck repeatedly by lightning bolts. "Soon. Hang on, darling."

Kevin opened the back door but Titus didn't speak as he stepped from the backseat and carried her quickly into the huge mansion where he took her up the winding staircase. Others of the tribe might be milling around but he paid no heed. Taking the stairs two at a time, he reached his suite of rooms in the west wing and went inside. Mahara make a panicked sound and sank her lips against his throat. He tightened his hold protectively.

By the time he reached the master suite, she was shaking like a leaf. A soldier stood nearby and rushed to fling open the heavy double doors and then shut them behind him. Candles of various shapes and sizes flickered around the dark room and he was pleased the females of his tribe had set the scene to his exact specifications. But now wasn't the time to admire their handiwork because Mahara was reaching crisis point and he could no longer prolong his claiming. Striding to the huge bed that dominated the center of the room, he laid her down tenderly and stripped her clothes from her body. Light from a feral moon filtered through the open balcony doors sending seductive shadows to dance through the room and shift over her nude body.

She was beautiful.

Titus caught his breath, held it as he drank her in. His body reacted violently to every lush curve. The raging erection he sported beneath the fabric of his slacks pulsed wildly in response to the sight of her. Unable to look away, he whipped his shirt, shoes and trousers from his body and felt his muscles ripple with the effort it took not to leap on her like the animal he was. Mahara lay sprawled across the backdrop of heavy dark blue satin, her hair spread like a dark fan across it. Her lush breasts heaved with each panting breath she took and Titus' mouth went dry at the sight of those pale pink nipples drawn tight.

Her waist was narrow, her hips full and shapely. Focusing his gaze on her smooth pussy he saw it was glistening with juice, seeping dew that dampened her inner thighs. Mahara's labia were swollen giving him a tantalizing glimpse of the pink petals of her weeping flesh. Suddenly her hips arched up and just like that, he was upon her. Yanking open her legs further, needing her, as a dark, heavy hunger lashed through his body, Titus buried his mouth against that tender flesh, felt it pulse meltingly against his tongue. Mahara cried out and lifted to meet his mouth as he sipped the cream from her body.

Her scent wound round him as he found her swollen clit with his mouth and sucked it, pulling and releasing gently. Keeping his mouth on the tender knot of nerves, he slid his fingers deep into her channel, finding her achingly hot and throbbing. The melting sweetness of her almost made him come without a single touch from her. Intense emotion lashed his senses, gripped his heart as the connection with this woman sank tender claws into his very psyche. Her sweet, hot cream poured over his plunging fingers to caress the broad palm of his hand. In. Out. In. Faster, harder, he finger-fucked her while drawing upon her clit.

Beneath him, she began to unravel at whirlwind speed and then she broke apart, coming against his eating mouth. Her fingers sank deep into his hair as she held on. His tongue went gentle on her flesh and her low moan swept through him like a benediction. Coming up on all fours, Titus crawled over her body and kissed her. Her answering sigh swept through his mouth and he buried his tongue deep, sharing her delicious taste. He nipped her lips, drank the heady warmth of his mate then sucked in a breath when he felt her small hand grip his cock.

"Gods!"

"Mm. You're gorgeous. The most gorgeous man I've ever seen," she murmured huskily. She made a fist around his pulsing shaft and squeezed gently. He wanted to tell her he wasn't a man but a great dark beast. It was too soon. She'd be terrified enough but the act of his claiming would help make things more clear. He would share himself, his thoughts and she would see his past. It was inevitable. The question remained, would she accept it?

Offering himself to her touch, he planted his knees next to her hips and rose up to loom over her. Rather than fear of what was happening to her, she seemed more curious than anything else. Every inch of his skin over muscle, bone and sinew was sensitized. Titus swore. "Look at me."

"How could I not? Just looking at you makes me hot."

A low growl rose up from his throat as she swept her hands up and down the length of his cock. "Touch my balls."

"Yes."

Titus watched her tongue dart out to stroke her bottom lip and he had to clench his teeth to maintain control over his body. Her fingers teased the heavy sac, played over that ultrasensitive flesh. Her thumb sought out the bundle of nerves behind his balls and pressed gently. His head started to spin. When she stroked again up the length of his shaft, he lost it. Throwing his head back, he gnashed his teeth and growled an inhuman sound. He was approaching the edge and his mate knew it.

Mahara felt the awful, beautiful heat sweep through her again. Her body ached in the most delicious ways and she wanted more and more and more. His hard cock fairly vibrated with each stroke of her hand and suddenly she wanted to taste him as he'd tasted her. Releasing him quickly, she pushed back with her elbows until she faced him on the bed. Lord, he was hard. Everywhere. Stillness held him and his strange golden eyes glittered with untamed lust as he watched her silently.

"Do you taste as good as you look?" she whispered, running curious fingers over the muscular mounds of his chest. "Bet you do, Titus."

She was surprised to see no hair on his body. Strange. But beautiful. Both hands trailed between his pecs and down his center and finally, she splayed them over his hard belly, loving the feel of him there. His cock brushed her wrist and she flicked her eyes up to meet his. "Do you, Titus? Do you taste as good as you look?"

Heat flashed in his eyes and tightened his feral features. Reaching lower, she cupped his pulsing erection and studied him. His nose was straight, proud with flaring nostrils as if he was smelling her, breathing her in. His high cheekbones were sharp slashes whose color was high with a lusty flush. Oh God! Those lips. Unable to resist testing their softness, still gripping his cock, she took lips that on a woman might be called lush. They were full and sculpted to absolute perfection, the bottom one slightly larger. A sexy dimple dented his chin. Nipping, she stroked that mouth, ate at it as he'd done with her as her hands worked his length. The low growl, the sounds he made seemed not quite human but that was ridiculous. "Suck my cock and find out," he said at last. His teeth were tightly closed and he seemed to struggle with each word.

Looking down at the big, purplish head, she noted its broadness, how thick it was. A drop of his seed glistened from the tip and Mahara bent to lap it up with her tongue. Above her, she heard Titus suck in a breath. That single sound galvanized her into action. She'd never been so turned on, so hot, so ravenous. She opened her mouth over the head and took it with tiny licks and strong pulls. Then she let him go, left him hanging to train her mouth slowly down the sides, feeling the heavy throbbing veins with her tongue. Lower she went to lick at his tight balls. She sucked them into the heat of her mouth as Titus made that strange coughing sound and buried his fingers in her hair. As if he'd willed it, her pussy gushed moisture that rained down her thighs and she whimpered against the hard flesh she caressed with her tongue.

His hips pumped and she took his cock again. Deeper. It brushed the back of her mouth and instinctively she relaxed her throat muscles to increase his pleasure. And hers. Pleasure and power surged hot and strong through her as her body wept for his taking. With a low sound, Titus withdrew from her mouth and grabbed her shoulders to push her back on the bed. His breath burst from his body in great blasts of sound and heat. Her own body responded wildly and she cried out when he grabbed her knees to spread her out, lift her, open her.

In a distant corner of her mind, she registered he didn't have a condom but it was as if he read her thoughts. "No need, sweet one. My kind doesn't carry disease."

His kind?

She'd barely registered the words when he buried his heavy erection deep into her core and she screamed at the power and fury of it. Tears pooled and drifted from her eyes at the sheer awesome pleasure. It was as if every nerve ending sat up and howled at the wicked sensation, the clamoring heat. Balanced on his heavily muscled arms, Titus began a slow plunge through overheated tissues and she could do nothing but writhe beneath his wild assault.

Slowly at first, he dragged his cock through her pussy, brushing every pleasure spot. Love, emotion, sexual excitement all balled up together, splintered out, then gathered her up. "Sweet little cat," he crooned. "My mate. My love."

His words rolled over her, sank in, buried deep with each thrust of his big body and then he quickened his pace and she couldn't think at all. Only feel. Sensations blasted through her like a quickly burning flame that threatened to render her a pile of ash. When he rotated his hips, grinding against her clit, she felt her body clench around his thick cock. He tensed above her for a nanosecond and pierced her with his gaze. Then he drove deep, plunging hard and faster than she'd ever known a person could move. The blasting sensations rocked her hard and she screamed her pleasure as she seemed to break into a million pieces. His teeth raked her nipples sending sensation up harder, higher. He sucked her nipple deep and she came again. Impossible.

"Yeah. Oh yeah."

Titus' words came at her as if from a distance as her body milked him. He blasted his seed deep inside her in great shots of heat. He jerked. His mouth opened to display a wicked pair of deadly fangs and a rasping sound burst from his throat. The muscles on his shoulders and those at his throat bunched like something else lived there beneath skin and bone.

A sense of wild unreality caught her up and she was outrageously turned on by the sight of him. Those fangs were pearly white and so dangerous-looking but she couldn't breathe, couldn't think. Impossibly, he stayed hard, still buried inside her. Even after coming as he had, the power he displayed was amazing. Inhuman.

Before she could draw breath, Titus pulled out of her body and buried his face against her throat. She felt those fangs scrap gently again her warm flesh, teasing at the pulse point and then he moved again, bringing that oddly tender scrape to the bud of her nipple before sucking it deep. Gasping her pleasure, she thought the fire that had burned so violently might be at an end but then it whipped hard through her once more. Mahara cried out. Sweat dappled her skin and her body seized.

"Again," she whispered. "Again. Oh, please."

The frantic words had no sooner been spoken when Titus rose over her to flip her to her stomach. A great heat tore up through her as more cream seeped from her willing body. She didn't care if he had fangs. She didn't care that Titus moved like a great hungry beast. She wanted him with every breath in her body. She'd lost track of the number of orgasms he'd given her but she wanted more. She was ravenous for them.

Mahara felt his hands on her hips as he lifted her to her knees. He grabbed her knees to widen her and she knew he would take her from behind. She was totally exposed to his gaze and she felt it trail over her back, her ass. His fingers dipped into her drenched folds, making her jerk and then she sighed as he spread the fluid higher and higher until he'd covered her anus with it. Circling the spot slowly, he slid his finger deep making her go still. "I'm going to fuck you here. Hard and deep. Gods, you're tight."

Alert to everything he did, she felt a dark pleasure draw her up when he sent another finger deep into her ass. One hand came up to stroke the length of her spine and settle, splayed, over the small of her back. The fingers inside her scissored deep several times and then he withdrew them. His tongue replaced his fingers as he dipped it inside to stroke her there and Mahara gasped at the sensation. He began to squeeze and pluck her clit in a slow lazy rhythm and a low sound broke free.

"Please. Oh, please. Titus."

He removed his tongue from her ass and nipped her pussy then she felt him move. The broad head of his cock settled between the cheeks of her butt, just at her opening and he gripped her hips. "Now. Now, Mahara."

Impossibly, he stretched her as he slowly entered. A delicious increment at a time he invaded her and the heavy, indescribable pleasure swept over her flesh, permeated that dark secret heart of her that she now realized had always been with her, buried deep inside. Motionless, she felt him fill her up as ever widening circles of pleasure burned low in her depths. Her belly clenched. When Titus bent over her back, sending his cock deeper than she could've ever imagined, she cried out. One hand came around and she watched with utter shock, as he touched the moon etched in the turquoise and silver ring. The silver magically moved and a tiny catch seemed to pop the stone from its setting. Titus took it in his fingers and she saw with amazement he held a matching turquoise stone in the palm of his hand. "My God!"

"You are meant to be my mate, Mahara. My stone and yours are exact matches. Feel them. Feel the energy."

She managed to touch both stones and felt them vibrating in unison, so hot, so beautiful. "Titus. What does it all mean?"

"It means you are mine, sweet one. From the exact minute of your birth, you have been mine and I've dreamed of this moment for a very long time. Feel the power now, love. Feel it. Let it draw you in while I take you."

Before she could blink, he placed the stones deep inside her pussy.

Vibrations, heat, power coursed low in her belly and blasted up through her core in quickening waves. Her nipples hardened and pulsed with an indescribable ache. Titus gripped her clit. She screamed as pleasure whipped hard and fast, as the wicked orgasm caught her up and then he began to move his cock deeply into her ass. A wild sound tore up from Titus' throat. Animalist. Feral.

Savage pleasure held her on a razor's edge as she bucked against him. He took her. Over and over as he kept her clit locked tight between his fingers. The stones buried in her cunt were moving together and she could feel the sparks of energy they sent zipping to every nerve, every pleasure zone. Vaguely, she realized she was sobbing.

She was coming, coming hard. Her body tightened, spiraled out of control with every plunge of his length in that forbidden place. She screamed and wailed. Suddenly, her hair was caught up in Titus' hands and he yanked her head back. He buried his fangs deep into her shoulder, just near her neck. The pleasure of it. The pain. The wild, wicked blast caught her up on a wave of orgasm she'd never experienced before. She'd never known ecstasy had a color but it did. It was turquoise blue and hot then cold. Powerful. The colors danced before her eyes, filled her mind and then clouded her perceptions of everything but the feel of his fangs buried deep, his body blasting through hers and then the colors faded and she saw nothing as she drifted into unconsciousness.

Chapter Three

୭

When she finally opened her eyes, it was to the feel of Titus carrying her in his arms. They entered the largest bathroom she'd ever seen. Black marble heavily veined with gold covered the wide floor and steam rolled up from the water in a huge black tub. A vague pain pulsed in her shoulder and she looked up at Titus. Despite what they'd shared together, his face was set in grim lines.

"Can you tell me what happened? What did you do to me?"

He caught her gaze and settled her slowly into the delicious warmth of the tub. Heat sank into her bones as he got in behind her and dragged her back against his chest. "I'll explain it all."

She sighed, leaned her head back on his shoulder, and looked up at him. "I'm not mad. It's weird. I should be completely freaked out but I'm not. I wonder why?"

Titus ran his hand over her shoulder, stopping briefly at his mark. "Perhaps you've always known you are different, hm?"

Nodding, she bit her bottom lip and looked off in the distance as reality sank in. More candles were lit in the darkened bathroom lending a mystical glow to the room. They flickered over the walls and she watched them for a moment before finally speaking out. "Mom told me when she died that it was time for me to find my destiny but then you know all about that, don't you."

"Yes. Natalie was a good woman but not of your blood. I personally placed you in her arms when you were a baby."

"Um. You aren't that much older than me, Titus. What are you? Maybe thirty-five, thirty-six?"

He laughed and pressed a kiss to the top of her head. "Hardly. I'm almost two hundred years old, Mahara."

"What? Are you a vampire or something?" Disbelief colored her words.

"Were-panther, darling. As you are."

Sitting up, she turned in his arms and looked at him aghast. "There's no such thing. I can't possibly be some kind of animal."

"You can and you are. And you are not just any animal, you are panther," he said with a tinge of satisfaction. "Your father was my first lieutenant, the best of men and your mother, Sara, was a were-panther hybrid who passed to you amazing psychic powers which should already be making an appearance in you."

Impossible. Crazy.

But the truth was hard to deny. She recalled the flashes of what she'd thought was intuition and began to wonder. Other things she'd seen and experienced tonight caused her to examine the facts. Titus had fangs for crying out loud! He'd bitten her during sex and she'd loved every second of it. And then there had been the wildfire of lust that had taken her over. The heat, the passion. It all made a weird sort of sense and the logical part of her mind took each fact out of its neat little compartment for further study.

Settling back again, she wondered about her parents. Did they not want her? "Where are they?"

"Your parents?"

"Yeah."

He let out a heavy breath. "They were murdered."

"Oh my God! Why?" Fury worked its way into her throat as she waited for his explanation. She'd never known them but the idea that she *could* have known them, loved them and been loved in return, filled her with a violence she'd never felt before.

"Everyone knew of Sara's gifts of prophecy but it had been assumed they couldn't have children. She and Galen hadn't been blessed with them but then suddenly you came along. I still remember it."

"You were there?" The very notion that he was present at the time of her birth was still shocking to her. Face it. It was weird.

He laughed. "Yes. You were beautiful then as you are now and your parents loved you more than life itself." Titus went serious and cupped her face. "Once word got around that a female were-panther hybrid had been born, other tribes around the world wanted you. One night Galen and Sara were hunting prey when they were attacked by several weres from Europe. They believed with Galen and Sara out of the way, they could take you and integrate you into their group."

"But you didn't let that happen."

"No."

"You wanted me for yourself."

"Yes, I did then and I do now. You were born into the Turquoise Moon tribe and are one of us." He pulled her wet body against his chest. Her breasts responded to the slight grazing and her breath hitched, her head swam with a passion unlike anything she'd felt before. "I've already claimed you," he murmured against her neck, caressing the bite with his tongue. "But you know it, don't you? You know it's true."

He was right. There was a scent to Titus, intoxicating, alluring and it was all over her too. Mahara's mind opened and she felt his feelings, knew his heart, realized without a doubt he was a man she could love through the ages of their lives. A peace settled deep inside and she now understood what Natalie Jones had been telling her from her deathbed. "The ring."

"It is a blessed ring, the one I wear and the matching one Natalie gave to you. They are a matched pair blessed by our forefathers from millennia past."

"Never thought I'd have a ring that vibrates. Handy."

Titus laughed uproariously and it positively transformed him. She noticed the stones had been replaced into their rings and assumed he'd taken care of business while she'd been passed out from all that great sex. Feeling suddenly free and yes, happy for the first time in years, she wrapped her arms around his neck and laughed with him. "Ah, Titus," she breathed. "You are an exciting man. I used to watch you walk down the hall and sigh over you."

His grin was bright and sudden. "Sweet. I'll confess too. I'd see you pass my door and get hard enough to hammer stone. The day you interviewed for personnel, I wanted to bend you over my desk and fuck you until you screamed for mercy." He swept his hands down her back and cupped her ass. "I wanted you then but I want you more now."

"Mm." Mahara nuzzled him, nipped his neck. "Am I supposed to bite you too? Does that seal the deal?" She shifted her body, moved her legs and planted her knees on either side of his hips then rose a bit from the water. His cock was rock hard and impulsively she took it in her hands loving the way he arched into them, the way his eyes darkened. His gaze zeroed in on her lips.

"You can bite me anytime, anywhere but it isn't necessary for our joining to be complete. You're mine, Mahara. For always. Have to admit though, the idea of you biting me makes we want to keep you in our bed forever."

"Not a bad idea. Are you sure we're…um…married?"

A dark brow lifted in question. "Do you want me to ask you in the human way?"

Feeling presumptuous and suddenly a little shy, she glanced down. "Um. I—"

"Marry me, Mahara," he whispered fiercely. Bending his head he nipped at her breast, then soothed with his tongue. "Live here with me and be my wife in every way."

Sweeping her hands through his black hair, she held him close as he sucked her nipple. Fire raced over her skin and her very center beat in time to her heart. Her pussy pulsed wildly as he sucked and teased. Her hands flexed on the steely hardness of his shaft and she could have brought him that way but that wasn't her plan. Teasing him, she removed her hands and watched him close his eyes to lean his head against the back of the tub. Smiling, she cupped water in her hands and poured it over him. Titus opened his eyes. Water clung to his black lashes like crystal drops and trailed down his cheeks. Reaching out, he picked up a bottle and thumbed open the lid. He motioned to her and she held out her hands to collect a fragrant measure of the soap. Immediately the scent of meadow grasses and sage filled the room.

Nothing flowery for this man.

Mahara noted he took some soap too and they watched each other as they rubbed their hands together until bubbles formed. As if they'd somehow become one person they moved together in the warm water, washing breasts, teasing, kissing. "Stand up," she whispered finally and when he complied, she moved her soapy hands over his lower body, soaping his strong warrior's thighs, dipping between to stroke his balls which were tight and hard from her touch. His cock rose proud and hard. She moved her hands over him, then rinsed before taking him deep into her mouth. As the warm water flowed around her waist she sucked and pulled. She stroked and played, loving the sounds he made and the way he fucked her mouth. Heat gathered, pooling between her thighs and she dipped one hand down to stroke her fingers through her flesh. Cream flowed thick over her fingers to finally blend into the water. Her clit was swollen, ultrasensitive and her breath broke when she pressed it.

Titus interrupted her play when he drew back with a groan and lifted up until she was standing before him. "My turn," he said, reaching out. He soaped her arms, her shoulder where his mark had turned dark purple, her throat. "You are beautiful."

Every touch of his warm hands sent pleasure spiking through her veins. Her thighs trembled as he reached between them to part her labia with his fingers. It was the most thorough washing she'd ever had and she wanted more. A low sound broke from her lips but it was like no sound she'd ever made before. Her eyes snapped open.

Titus reached out to steady her. "Sh. Easy, love."

Mahara stared at him aghast. Her gums tingled and it felt as if her blood heated to unbearable heights. Her flesh felt tight too tight for her body. "What's happening?"

"Come," he said. "It's time but I'll help you through it."

Panic set in but she stood mutely while Titus rinsed the soap from her body. Within seconds he dried her with a fluffy black towel and led her back into the bedroom. Titus turned to her. "I'm going to change for you. If you see it maybe you won't be quite so afraid."

"Afraid?" she panted. "I'm scared spitless. Does it hurt?"

He shook his head. "It's just disconcerting at first. You get used to it and after awhile you will love being in your cat form. It's exhilarating and like nothing you've ever experienced before."

"You don't have to convince me of that. Never in my wildest dreams did I imagine anything like this. And your little pep talk didn't work, Titus. I'm still scared."

"There's more and you must know, this is part of how we bring a queen into her change."

"We?"

A muscle flexed in his jaw but he didn't speak. He closed his eyes and, to her utter amazement, there was a shifting of muscle beneath his skin that was beyond strange. Something alive and wild seemed to live there, deep inside him. Then and there, he began to shift into his other self. Paws complete with sharp claws appeared, fur grew as if by magic over his skin. It was the most amazing thing she'd ever seen and it happened so quickly it stunned her.

Her ass hit the bed and she blinked at the huge, glossy panther with eyes of molten gold. Her hands went up over her mouth as she stood and warily moved closer. "Titus?"

Titus flashed his fangs and made that coughing sound she'd heard before. He was a huge, muscular animal and so gorgeous, tears burned behind her eyes. Tentatively she reached for him, watched him close those spooky eyes and then sank her fingers into his shiny coat. She would look like him. Her mind flashed with images that came to her at warp speed. His past, his present and her part in it all. She saw her parents as he'd known them and witnessed her birth.

Consumed with emotion, she buried her face against his strong neck and breathed him in. Tears burned sharp and her body reacted to changes she had only now begun to accept. Without warning, he switched to his human form and gathered her close. "This is what you will become. I have claimed you as my mate but there is more to do before you can change. The signs of your other half trying to break free are upon you, sweet one and it is your destiny to be my queen. For that to occur a level of worship must happen."

"I don't want to be worshiped," she whispered. "I don't."

Titus picked her up and carried her to the bed and gently laid her in the center. Joining her, he leaned over and brushed her hair back with one hand. "Your father learned with your mother that her psychic powers combined with everything else required more in the way of passion. That will be the case with you, darling."

"I don't understand any of this," she whimpered as his hand began to play in the folds of her sex. She felt the force of leashed energy rise up again, sharp and wild, stronger than it had been before. When he plucked her clit until it was a swollen, throbbing mass, her back arched and a fine trembling attacked her body. His mouth found her nipple. The sucking was stronger this time. Titus' fangs scraped against them almost painfully but she loved it. It lit a raging fire deep in her belly. Her hands found his shoulders and when she used her nails lightly on his skin, his groan of pleasure fueled her desire.

"Fuck me. Fuck me now."

"In time," he murmured against her breast before sucking deeply again. He plunged three fingers deep into her channel and she cried out sharply, needing more, needing everything her body could take. Suddenly she jerked at several wild sounds and she turned to see two panthers prowling through the open balcony doors. "Kevin. Samuel. It's good you're here."

Mahara watched in amazement as the panthers formed into the bodies of perfectly beautiful naked men. One she vaguely recognized as the man who'd driven the limo. The other, stunningly handsome with long wavy brown hair, was a stranger. Kevin approached the bed, looking like a great blond warrior, with his long hair and austere features. Mahara felt her pussy weep. A sharp ache of sexual pleasure ran wicked fingers over her flesh.

"We could be nowhere else in our lady's time of need. We are here to serve," he said with a nod.

Titus removed his hand from her body and she felt the loss of his touch instantly. She whimpered as that terrifying lust beat savagely in her chest, between her legs. Centering her focus on the newcomers, she was oddly accepting of their presence. Who was she kidding? She knew why they were here and was ready for anything they had to give her. She loved Titus. She did. But the needs of her body couldn't be denied.

Samuel approached her first and kneeled upon the bed to give her a chaste kiss on her lips. His brown eyes were soulful as he smiled. "You honor us, Queen. I will lay down my life for you."

After a nod from Titus, Kevin did the same and kneeled naked next to Samuel on the bed. Mahara expected a kiss on the lips as Samuel had done but he surprised her by taking her nipple into his mouth. His suck was a sharp rasp, he drew deeply and she felt her body weep violently. Yes! Oh, dear God! Yes! When he released her nipple, his eyes were full of passion and need. "You honor us. Let us help you come into your true self."

"Yes," she whispered but she wasn't certain anyone heard because the men were suddenly upon her. Growls and low moans swirled in the air around her as Kevin returned to her nipple. Titus kissed her lips then took the other in his warm mouth. From below she felt her legs being spread wide.

"You are lovely here, my queen," Samuel said. She felt the stroke of his fingers through the drenched petals of her sex, felt the cream seep from her depths. He cupped her ass and the sensation of his long hair brushed against her thighs was delicious. Samuel's breath was hot. Then he opened his mouth and took her cunt with his teeth and tongue and lips. His tongue licked over her clit and sucked it deep.

As Samuel ate her out, Titus' hand swept her belly then went further to lift one knee to open her to Samuel's touch more fully. Kevin did the same. She'd never, ever been more exposed or felt more vulnerable. Titus released her breast and moved. She felt him reach out to remove the smoldering turquoise from her ring but then she couldn't think at all because Kevin was now clutching both of her breasts, moving from one to the other, to lick and suck.

Titus sent his fingers between the cheeks of her ass and probed lightly. Heat and a sizzling, electrifying energy pulsed up from the place and shimmered through her. She felt the insertion of the vibrating stones and caught her breath. Titus was suddenly there, at her lips, tasting them as Samuel drank cream from her pussy. Samuel drew strongly from her clit as the hot stones rubbed deep inside her and Titus kissed her as she broke. The orgasm blasted through her, catching her up, holding her on a sharp peak.

But she had little time to come down.

Her experience was far from over.

Chapter Four

Titus lay beside her as Kevin released her breasts and moved to the foot of the bed. Gently, Titus pulled her over his body and brought her hips down over his engorged cock. Sensation spiked again, rumbling through her like an avalanche. Unbelievably, she was ready for another orgasm. She needed it. The feel of Titus filling her, stretching her was unbearably sweet, erotic in an over-the-top way she'd never felt before. A conflagration of emotion swept her as he lifted his hips to go deeper.

Samuel moved to her side and looked at her with those solemn brown eyes. His erection was huge and pulsing, glistening at the tip with his seed. His hunger called to her and she needed to feed it. He took his cock in his hand and dragged it slowly up and down. His eyes drifted shut. Mahara glanced at Titus and saw acceptance in his eyes. "He belongs to you."

"Yes," she murmured as she turned her head and took Samuel's cock in her mouth to suck. His low moan filled her with a deeper need and she began to move on Titus, loving the feel of him buried deep inside her sweltering pussy.

Kevin reappeared into the scene when she felt his fingers probe her ass. He dipped with his fingers and she felt the loss of the stone's heat. While she sucked Samuel and enjoyed Titus' strong fucking, she heard a click near the bedside table and knew he'd put the beautiful turquoise away. She heard the sliding of a drawer and then Kevin moved to her backside again. Something warm was spread around her anus and she felt Kevin's finger glide inside. "You are so tight here, Queen."

Her mouth was full. She couldn't respond but Titus chose that moment to latch onto her swollen nipple as Kevin probed her ass with the head of his cock. She stilled as he slid inside and pushed her lower until she lay upon Titus chest. Samuel sank one hand into her hair as he fucked her mouth with smooth, slow strokes. Behind her, Kevin groaned loudly, made a wicked, coughing sound.

Mahara realized these men filled her everywhere. It was crazy but she loved it. Titus' hands swept her sides as if to gentle her. Kevin's chest rested on her back as she continued sucking Samuel who increased his pace. She heard his low growl. Opening her eyes, she saw his face had grown taut with passion and she felt the need in him. He had to come and tried to pull from her mouth but she shook her head wildly.

Stay.

The word was a whisper in her mind but Samuel heard it. She knew he did. "Yes. Oh yes, my queen."

Without any other warning he blasted his cum into her mouth and she drank it down, loving the taste of him. Titus and Kevin had gone motionless but when Samuel slumped onto the bed, they began to move in tandem. Titus from below and Kevin, from behind. Stretched to the utter limit, Mahara absorbed every sensation, every quiver. They parried and withdrew leaving her constantly filled. Kevin groaned and nipped her shoulder blade as Titus latched onto a nipple. Heat tore, ripped, wound tight and she wailed at the sensations that were more erotic than anything she'd ever experienced. The razor's edge on which she was held was sharp, steep. Each movement by the man behind her and her love beneath her, threatened to send her toppling into an abyss and then it came. Wailing out, weeping, she stiffened and then stumbled off the precipice carried on a cloud of color and light.

"Now?" The harshly gritted question came from Kevin.

"Yes. Now! Gods, yes!" Titus growled it out, imperious and sharp as he blasted into her depths. Kevin stiffened and came too, coming in her ass with great, hot spurts. Mahara was carried up and over another sharp edge as Titus crooned nonsensical love words against her breast. Both men withdrew and the instant loss of them made her want to howl despite the shattering orgasm she'd had. When Kevin moved away, Titus rolled with her until her back lay against the cool satin spread.

He settled his head in the crook of her neck and pressed his lips against her overheated skin. She didn't know what the other men were doing but then she felt their hands on her limp body. Both held warm cloths and were lazily washing her. Kevin swept the cloth between her butt cheeks and through the folds of her pussy. Samuel paid special attention to her arms and belly as he pampered her.

When she studied Samuel, a great affection bloomed in her chest. He belonged to her. He was a part of her as much as Titus. He looked up and smiled then took her hand and pressed a kiss to the back of it. "Thank you, my lady."

"Oh, Samuel. Thank *you*."

Kevin, whom she had discovered wasn't as sensitive in nature, looked down at her, the wet cloth held in one hand. He smiled and bowed his head. "Thank you for sharing your pleasure with us. We are your servants."

"Once again," Titus said. "Your service to the new queen is indispensable but you must stay for the transition. Already I feel the beast rising in her again."

He was right!

Heat tore up, lashing her with a swiftness that stole her breath. Could she stand to be fucked again? Could she tolerate what was sure to come? Again her gums tingled and her pussy gushed cream. A wild inhuman cry lashed up through her throat and as if from a distance, she felt the men move. Her wrists were tied together, by Kevin, she thought. Samuel raced to the foot of the bed and she heard the sound of something tearing. The sheets? Her ankles were lashed to either post at the foot of the bed. Titus came over her and loomed there.

As if seeking to reclaim her sanity in any way she could, she stared up into his beautiful eyes and saw a tiny smile settle on his lips. "Don't be afraid. I'm here and I love you beyond all things. Let yourself go, Mahara."

She knew she had no choice in the matter. Lust beat with wicked wings through her body, her clit pulsed and when Titus sank his fingers deep into her channel she felt those overused tissues fill with renewed desire, clutching at his fingers but needing more.

Her fingers, held above her by restraints, curled, as she sought to break free, needing to touch Titus but it was impossible. She was stretched taut beneath him. Naked, Titus balanced himself on his knees and fisted his hand around his cock. It had grown to enormous proportions and she glimpsed a hint of fangs. When he dragged his fist over his erection, saw that broad head grow bright with color, she felt fangs burst from her gums and she hissed at him.

Titus made a returning sound and buried himself hard and deep in her sheath. Someone slipped a pillow beneath her ass to lift her for his claiming and she snapped her teeth in response. She almost itched for his cock, the ache growing stronger and stronger, propelling her upward as she clutched and released, clutched and released.

He gnashed his teeth, snapping wildly and suddenly he withdrew to sink his teeth into the tender notch between her thigh and her pussy. A feral scream broke from her. His tongue was rough on her clit. Rough like a cat's, like sandpaper almost and she came with a fury as her legs jerked spasmodically against the bonds around her ankles. Then Titus was back, fucking her wildly, each thrust inching her higher and higher. His eyes seemed different. Wilder, the pupils slanted rather than round. He bared his teeth and bit at her breast and her neck.

She struck then. Like an animal, she struck and sank her teeth into his shoulder. He jerked and howled, pumping deep, driving hard, sending pleasure on a crash and burn mission through her pussy. "Yes," he shouted. "Yes."

He stiffened as she splintered into a million pieces. Her body seized and in that moment she felt his emotions, his love for her. She felt every moment of loneliness and the way he'd ached for the day she'd become his. Emotion, sexual pleasure, flashed up to illuminate her world and the blast of love grabbed deep as she flew apart beneath him.

When Titus withdrew from her body, they were alone.

The male were-panthers had apparently left the way they'd come in but she couldn't think about that now. She was changing. Everything was changing and it wasn't painful. It was beautiful. Mahara felt her flesh ripple and knew somehow she was seeing the world for the first time through a panther's eyes. She watched, as an eerie calm settled her, her flesh turned to a smooth, lush coat of silky black fur. Instinctively, she leaned her head forward to lick her paw and noted the presence of lethal claws.

At the foot of the bed lay her mate, a great beast, who stared at her with golden eyes. She crept forward and nuzzled his big neck then leapt from the bed anxious to try her new kitten feet. He followed and together they went through the balcony doors and into the night. At the end of the balcony, was a set of wide steps that led onto an elaborately manicured lawn and further beyond was a lush, green forest. A feeling of exhilaration, of utter joy filled her as they raced together, him taking the lead.

Mahara wasn't sure how long they played but finally she followed him to a clear stream deep in the woods that sifted musically over rocks and pebbles. The grass there was thick and lush. Titus lapped at the water then turned his great head.

You converted beautifully but then I knew you would.

You're speaking in my head.

And you are speaking in mine. It is the way of mates and that is what we are. Forever.

Now that I'm in this form, she thought. *How do I change back?*

Instantly Titus, shifted and changed, taking form as a gloriously naked man. He reached down and laid his hand on her head. "Imagine it. It's easy."

Mahara hissed at his words. Yeah, right. Typical that he'd think everything should be easy. She was new to this. But she allowed the image of her human self to flash through her mind and she began to change. It happened so fast she barely had time to blink and then she was standing there, as naked as he, grinning at him. "Wow."

Titus came up to her and drew her down with him onto the thick, cool grass. "Wow is right," he smiled, stroking her bare belly.

As the night moved mysterious and dark around them, they talked until finally she came back to the millions of questions she had about her past, her parents and her new life. "I wish I'd known my parents," she whispered as he teased her lips with a blade of grass. "Do you think they'd have loved me?"

"They did. They gave their lives to protect you. It's the way of our people but even more so when applied to children. They adored you."

"I always wondered about my name. Did they name me or did Natalie? I've never heard it before and now I want to know."

Titus shifted and came up over her. His eyes seemed to burn with golden fire and she felt herself drawn into them "They didn't name you, Mahara. Neither did, Natalie. I was the one who named you, my love."

Unable to stop herself, she reached up and stroked his face, loving him beyond measure. "What does it mean, Titus? What does Mahara mean?"

He kissed her then, long and slow and she felt his love take her over, body and soul. "I named you Mahara for what you mean to me. *My heart.*"

Back in the bedroom, two stones lay side by side, touching slightly. Heat sizzled through them, connecting them to the two lovers who lay together under a feral moon.

VEINS OF TURQUOISE
Elaine Lowe

જી

Dedication

Thanks to Mary Claypool, Yutaka Omatsu, Yoshiki Sakurai, Dai Sato and Shotaro Suga for inspiration and a vision of the future that is liberating and terrifying all at once.

Thanks to Larry, for always being supportive and being my own personal hero.

Author's Note

The colors of turquoise speak of the exotic. The name itself comes from the country Turkey, not the place of origin of the stone but for Europeans, the place through which they got their supplies. The true source of the stone is great dry plains of Persia or the desert of the Sinai. Now, we see turquoise from the high arid plateaus of the American southwest and the hinterland of China. A stone formed frequently in the desert, turquoise speaks of the memory of water, and life in the wasteland.

Always, the color makes you sit up and take notice, whether it's the blue of the sky or the green of the stormy sea. Those stunning colors come from the copper and iron within the stone. Many cultures consider those vibrant colors to be signs of wealth. In Tibet and China, the stone is a measure of the wearer's health and subtle changes in the color of the stone are interpreted as reflecting changes in the owner. Among the Navajo, turquoise was a piece of the sky fallen to earth and one of the most sacred stones known. Turquoise is still valued for its ability to promote communication and understanding.

Chapter One
Dancing Alone

☙

The pulsing music of the party surrounded her, sweeping her heart rate higher as her body contorted through movements that were physiologically impossible. The Hyvan flute battled with the keening of Mdinan underwater chants and the frantic thrumming of Eadosian kettle drums. Not much sonic room left for the weak, willowy synthesized singer to fill, fortunately.

Lights flashed in shades of ultraviolet and infrared onto the dancing crowd of humans every color of the rainbow. Here, on the Tessnet, physiology was only the starting point for imagination. There were some dancers with kaleidoscopic skin, others with unbelievably silky lilac hair or a ridiculously stiff metallic silver mane. Add to the mix avatars prancing by as unicorns, or swooping overhead as Qsakian flying mantas or swimming through the crowd as cetaleans or giant Killian sunfish. Then there were hoots and growls, the whoops and melodic alien trills.

Really, just another typical Tessnet virtual reality rave.

The Galactic Tesseract Internetwork System was known far and wide simply as the Tessnet. Everyone spent at least some time here, though it was strictly regulated for fear of addiction or insanity. There were a few illegal Tessaddicts in the node even now and Galita Serhadze could smell their desperation. She knew that the Galactic Corporate Attorneys' techhounds were likely hard on their code trail. Sighing, she realized she was no longer titillated by the sense of danger at such an event. Instead of observing the coming chase, she drifted to the edges of the node and looked out at the flashing tubes of cyberspace on the Tessnet. The shifting lights were her own brain's interpretation of the information landscape outside the rave node she'd loaded herself into an hour ago.

Maybe it was a nanosecond slower transfer speed since her body was on Lithos I, outside the central core of Tessnet nodes, but overall she just seemed discontent lately with her usual net haunts. Dancing, games, music, even flirtation seemed stilted and hollow.

"Home." There was a whisper, crystal clear in her mind despite the loud ambient din of the node. The voice was soft, deep and comforting but it was also utterly alien, with layers of age and wisdom beyond anything she could imagine. Was it her own mind playing tricks on her?

Extremely well-paid experts had just gotten through putting her brain through the most rigorous psychological examinations in the galaxy. She'd passed with flying colors, as she had done every two years, keeping her license as an Information Engineer, with all of her clearances and Tessnet privileges. The GCA was willing to bet a lot of time and money on the fact that she did not have a tendency to go insane. If she heard a voice, it was real.

But the voice spoke no longer. Whatever program that had triggered it and gotten past her firewall had let her be. Strangely, she felt the ache of its loss. She was missing something and had been for a long time.

She decided to try to trace through its echo but just as she prepared to enter the dive portal for the node to find the rapidly disappearing datastream, a huge avatar stepped in front of her, putting a halt to her movement. She looked up at a man who had definitely tried too hard to appear as a sex god and therefore completely failed.

As he was close to two and a half metras tall, she had to stare up at him. *Oh, he promises a whole eight and a half minutes of fun before somebody makes a mess and falls asleep.* His chest was like a barrel, pecs glistening with oil, a waist so narrow that overall he looked triangular. He couldn't stop at designing six or twelve abdominal muscles. Oh no, this fellow decided that sixteen were a good idea. Massive thighs the size of Hyvanian hams, ridiculously huge feet that a normal human would have tripped over. At least the bulging equipment was packaged up in a tiny glow-in-the-dark bikini.

His face was not an improvement. Long midnight blue hair framed a chiseled face with perfect pouting lips. Just like every other avatar of the sexually desperate, this guy did try to do something distinctive though—he'd pasted on an eyepatch to the standard "alpha-male" Tessnet avatar preprogrammed package. She supposed it was to give the appearance of "danger" to the oiled-up cretin. For her, it screamed "pirate" and after the rape of her home ship, the DMTR, by Karogian pirates some eight months previously, she was in no mood to humor any idiot looking like something she loathed.

"Hey, sugar tits. Wanna have some fun tonight?" Oh, the voice program wasn't a good match at all, at least an octave too high for the size of that chest. Tsk-tsk. Galita hated shoddy workmanship.

She didn't even want to acknowledge the ass who had cost her the chance to trace that voice she'd heard but before she could maneuver around him in virtual space, she felt the sensation of rough hands trying to grab her ass. The guy was motionless except for a lurid smirk but he was trying to break through her firewalls to cop a feel! He was doing a rotten job of it too, as it felt more like pins and needles than anything lascivious, much less sensuous.

Narrowing her eyes, she sent back a hard jolt straight to the groin, shattering the creep's firewalls and causing the man-god in front of her to flicker into a greasy little man a good metra shorter than she was, curled up in pain. He looked like an accountant from some high-rise office building on Mitka II who hadn't seen the dim sun outside for a decade or so. *Blech.*

Blowing out a virtual breath, she brushed past her conquest to enter a dive portal and so returned to the local entry room on Lithos. She spent a moment trying to decide whether to go virtual sandskiing on Fardo III or just enter sleep mode and dwell on the lingering discontent in her dreams.

Deciding on neither, she opened her eyes—her real, boring, brown eyes—and returned to her body. The Lithos room was strangely comforting, for all its plain, utilitarian décor. Old-fashioned anti-grav couches cushioned the body and applied the subtle pressure waves that prevented her muscles from atrophying while she was diving. A background of white noise teased the eardrums into staying flexible. The nutritional and waste needs were met with subtle ear clips rather than messy tubing like in some older facilities. Overall, she was pleased with the place. Deciding to exercise her real body rather than leaving it to the med programs she swung out her legs from the too high couch and hopped onto the floor. One thing about these Lithians, contrary to physics, they decided to grow ridiculously tall despite the heavy gravity on the planet. Her own long Phytos legs looked pathetically short in comparison with any Lithian female she'd met. And the men! Oh, they were impressive.

Galita smiled as she exited the room. The pressure controlled door closed with a hiss behind her and she entered one of the standard rock-carved halls of most buildings she'd seen on Lithos. Molded crylic was just not in fashion here and really, she couldn't blame the designers. Stone definitely had a solid, permanent feel. Maybe it was a bit drafty at times but truly, it felt good to have everything not be absolutely perfect all the time. If she wanted that, she could stay in the Tessnet.

She laughed in wry amusement and a wave of blue rippled across her skin, disturbing the light green she had settled on that morning. Unlike most Phytos, Galita had conscious control over the color cells in her phytodermis. If she wanted to be pale rose one day and robin's-egg blue the next, she didn't have to trick her skin with altering the light she was exposed to, Galita could change at will. It was a rare ability but one she liked to have fun with. Polka dots and stripes were a good conversation starter and, if angry, she could always announce her displeasure with a well-chosen insult appearing somewhere on her skin.

She'd been good enough that when she was in college, the GCA tried to recruit her to their Covert Division. Fortunately she hadn't been so good that they would have made it an offer she couldn't refuse. Besides, she had one problem that meant she could never completely blend into the background — she could change the tone of her skin easily enough but the bright red of her hair was irrepressible. Even the best and most expensive of dyes and genetic treatments seemed to be rejected by her body and she was doomed to life as a redhead, no matter what color her skin was.

Mostly, this particular talent, changing her skin at will and whim, it was just part of who she was, like her talent for diving the Tessnet. It always made her look deeper than the surface. And Lithos, she just hadn't quite figured out yet.

Maybe she would soon. Many of her shipmates seemed remarkably content, given what little choice they had in coming here. The plague on DMTR had attacked the oldest crewmembers first. Galita herself was young and healthy enough that she could have chosen alternative treatment but the experience of symbiosis with a silicon life form seemed too amazing, too novel, to say no. So, she'd eaten her juicy pomegranate seeds and become host to the tiny symbiotes of Lithos.

So far, she'd not really had the opportunity to enjoy any differences, other than the slow burning ache that had plagued her during her testing on Mars. The disappearance of that ache once she got to Lithos was a visceral pleasure, the kind she had rarely felt in her true body. It made her crave other sensations. She'd never tasted Mdinan lobster, only the electronic version passed into her sensory neurons. She'd never inhaled the sweet air at the top of the Skilani Range of Eados V, only the simulated kind. And for all her acrobatic, encyclopedic knowledge of sex and the thousands of partners she'd enjoyed and discarded, she'd never felt the heat of a man's cock inside her own flesh. All in all, she realized that she was falling into the Tessnet pit that all InfoEngs had to avoid at all costs, to have more of herself embedded in the net than in her own brain. Otherwise someday she could dive in and never come back up again.

She paused to look out the bank of windows lining the Entry Room building. The circular hallway encompassed a garden at the center, one of the hundreds that seemed scattered like shiny pebbles across the central city of Arott. They were beautiful places, very different from the chaotic lushness of the growth on board DMTR. Restrained but still full of life, just life very different from anything else she'd seen in the galaxy. The strange blend of hard and soft in shalemoss, or the fragile crystalline blooms of a starflower. Each garden she'd visited was a different adventure for the senses. This particular one though, held a completely different allure.

He was there again. Sitting on the bench in the rock garden in the cold, thin Lithian air and facing the windows in the hallway where she stood. He seemed to be there every time she exited the Arollian Tessnet Center in this state of discontent. Either he was following her with illegal psi skills, had hacked into her personal locator code or was somehow the source of that discontent. Then again, perhaps it was just wishful thinking involving a prime example of Lithian male.

Galita hadn't really understood Matrissa's obsession with Lithos. Sure, Rissa had acquired the finest male specimen Galita had seen live in her short forty-five years, so the good doctor had motivation to like this strange barren planet. If Irav Tok had been single or mated to any other woman in the galaxy, Galita would have taken a retinal scan and within five minutes of catching sight of his perfectly luscious body and sufficient privacy, she'd have had a simulation of the man filling every orifice of her body to her intense simulated satisfaction.

Unfortunately, Irav happened to be claimed by the woman who was Galita's best friend in the galaxy and Galita couldn't help feeling that sex, even virtual sex, with a simulacrum of her best friend's mate was not a good idea. It had all the trappings of a bad Tessdrama episode.

Galita had refused to believe that more men like Irav could exist on this backwater planet. She'd had to stay in the Sol system when DMTR had come back to Lithos, spending two months on Mars for her testing. By the time she'd finally arrived on Lithos by freighter, the constant longing for something indefinable had scratched like a horrible itch. Upon setting foot on the ground and breathing in the cold, crisp air of the main city, Aroll, the itch had faded, replaced by intense curiosity.

She'd been here for three weeks now and the place constantly surprised her. Her current obsession, the man looking so intently in her direction. It turned out Irav was not unique at all. This man, the one who stared at her with those vivid blue eyes, made any fantasies of Irav Tok disappear like a vapor. What was it in the air around here that produced such men? Real, flesh and blood men, not designed in some avatar-specialty lab. Those eyes were the most brilliant shade of blue, such a vibrant color that she wondered if they were a gene-alt. But he just didn't seem the type, as serious and grave as his expression always appeared.

In fact, he wasn't her type at all, although her body was screaming the opposite—her nipples tight, her pupils dilated, her pussy slick in readiness. He was a redhead! She hated red hair. But really, on him it worked. His skin was a warm, rich brown tinged with red, like the weathered limestone in the deserts of old Earth or the dry, dusty plains left in the non-terraformed reserves on Mars. His hair was just a shade lighter, more a deep rust than brown. His arms were things of beauty and she resented the thin sleeveless shirt that covered his chest from her perusal. She wondered how his skin would taste if she ran her tongue across the muscles of that chest—if his stomach would flutter as her mouth descended, if his cock would be warm and hard in her mouth and what his scent would be like in her nostrils. She didn't want to rush off to make a simulation of this man. She wanted him, real and live and entwined with her in hot sweaty glory.

For Infinity's sake! The man was looking right at her. He was still some five metras away and she knew that these floor-to-ceiling windows were one way, that it was impossible to see inside the crylic window from that bench. But his eyes perused the length of her body, making her swallow nervously and bite the fullness of her lower lip. Her folds felt heavy and full, her temperature seemed to soar and she could feel her phytoderm ripple in an effort to harness the sudden hormonal changes into a store of energy. Ah, to be a Phytos, ever-mindful of limited resources. It was then that she noticed her hand pressed against the crylic of the window—the skin that was quickly becoming the same shade of deep red-brown as the man watching her from outside. The color crept down her arm and had almost made it past her elbow before she wrenched her hand away from the window and shook it vigorously, forcing it back to the green it had been a moment before. She hadn't changed her phytodermis unconsciously since she'd been a teenager! What in Infinity was happening to her?

"Happy to be home, Galita Serhadze?" A voice was speaking in her mind again but this voice was gravelly and utterly human. A voice full of challenge and temptation. "Is this finally home?"

She wanted to scream back but she didn't know what the hell he was asking, much less what she should answer. And she knew, beyond a shadow of a doubt, that the voice belonged to the man sitting outside—well, he had been sitting outside. While she had been raging internally, trying frantically to find the hole in her firewalls and wireless comm that he'd exploited to access her audio receptors, he'd simply walked away. Damn that infuriating man, Mardon Kaen. And damn her for wanting him.

If a woman was finally, finally going to pick a man to be her first bio-partner for sex, why did the guy have to be so damn mysterious!

Then she was overcome by an image so strong she sank to her knees right there in the public hallway, lost to everything but sensation.

Was she in the Tessnet? Was she asleep? Did it matter when she felt like this? Her skin was electrified – every nerve ending was receiving nothing but bliss. Behind her knee, it was the whisper of a hot breath. Along the curve of her breast, the lightest teasing touch of a single finger. On the inside of her thigh, the firm but gentle bite of teeth. Her breath came in shuddering gasps and her eyes darted around the smooth brilliance surrounding her. She was trapped in the warm heart of a sunset, light she couldn't block out even when she closed her eyes. It shone within her, through her, not letting her hide anymore from her own insecurities, her own sexuality.

She reached her hands out, pleading for something to hold on to and he was there, wrapped in her arms, his lips whispering promises against her neck that she couldn't understand but they stirred fire that sang through her blood. Her legs wrapped around his hips and he slid inside her easily, filling her like no program, no simulation, no cybersex partner had ever come close to doing. He wasn't just triggering neurons in her cortex, he was making her body sing. She didn't know which direction was up and whether they were on a bed, the floor or floating in liquid gold but nothing mattered but the friction of his cock within her sheath, the completion of being filled where she hadn't realized she was empty.

Her pussy clamped around him, holding him within her, making it as difficult as possible for him to withdraw. But oh, when he did, when he slammed back inside, it was the sweetest homecoming imaginable. His lips sucked each nipple into his mouth in turn, nipping them and driving her into a higher state of frantic desire. Their hips slammed together, his hands spanning her ass and pushing them against each other with greater and greater energy until she felt like they were going to combust. When those blue-green luminescent eyes stared into hers, she did.

When she came, she opened her mouth in a silent scream, raking nails down his back as she felt him explode within her. Light exploded behind her eyes and she closed them in reflex.

When she opened them, she was shaking on all fours in a cold stone hallway, alone.

"Risheva. Come to Risheva, Galita Serhadze."

Oh, damn him for a zit on a *tralc*'s ass. Why all the damn mystery for Infinity's sake?

Chapter Two
Finding a Partner

The wind sighed across the ravines of Risheva whistling a unique tune that Mardon Kaen knew like the back of his hand. The swirling sounds were a comfort to him, though others had described the sound as haunting, even desolate. They weren't listening to Lithos. Not like he did.

Not that he always wanted to listen. His instinct had sent him to Aroll and he was happy to return from what seemed like a fool's errand. No off-world weedpelt was going to hear things that he himself couldn't. Yes, the veins had been particularly active lately. Yes, not one of the members of the Miners Union could understand the meaning behind the insistent feeling of frustration that the planet seemed to throb with lately. Not even Mardon, with his exclusive, advanced Information Engineer enhancements and history of electronic symbiosis, could understand the order within the chaos of the copper veins of Lithos. There was only one person he'd ever thought might be able to help.

But he didn't know whether he was thinking rationally or whether it was his cock talking.

Galita Serhadze was far too young for him. He knew her entire profile, because he'd been one of the examiners for her latest round of license testing. He knew she was barely forty-five, almost a child compared to his one hundred-and-sixty-two years in the galaxy. He'd been an InfoEng more than twice as long as this little girl had been alive. He had no business wanting to know what her throbbing clit would taste like on his tongue, or the screams she would make when she climaxed around his cock. And he was quite certain she would be a screamer.

He'd never met her face-to-face on Mars. Only through the thick shielding that separated the test subject from the examiner. She passed through every psychological test with amazing ease. The clarity of her thought, of her ability to separate fantasy and reality, was remarkable. It was almost as though she could detect the very fabric of reality, on the edge of some kind of psi ability but one he had never heard of. He was convinced that she would be able to discover whether the pulses emanating from the depths of Lithos into the Mines of Risheva were merely the result of seismic action, or something much, much more profound.

If only he could manage to restrain his desire to ravish her long enough to convince her that he wasn't insane. His back still stung from the ghostly imprint of her nails raking it as she came. It had been the height of stupidity to take her—practically to rape her like that—but he could feel her desire flowing off her like waves. Her firewalls were rock solid but he still had the Information Department's break-down codes for emergencies during testing. He'd shamelessly used them to lure her in and the lust-filled nature of her thoughts had been too much to resist.

Now, he wanted more. He wanted to lick every cetar of her fascinating skin and feel the unique texture of phytodermis against his tongue. He wanted to explore every facet of her imagination, both in the Tessnet and in the flesh. He wanted to think he'd be able to restrain himself from exploding inside her the minute he thrust inside but he was not at all certain of his abilities. She was just too damn hot.

Was he losing it? His own licensing requirements were spaced every ten years and he wasn't due for another round for another three years. But between his obsession with the voices and sensations reported by people in the old Risheva mine and in other areas of high-copper concentration, he thought he was exploring a unique trait of Lithos. When had he crossed over from scientist to believer? Did he have a right to lure this beautiful girl into his world? Would she simply report him to the Information Department and have him stripped of his rights?

For some reason, he wasn't sure whether it was his mind or his cock that made the decision but he trusted her. He'd given her a task — would she follow through?

In the distance, silhouetted against the dark horizon under the ever-present sun high in the sky, a gravsled was moving over the rocky terrain in a slow, methodical pattern of search. He felt a soft, skillful ping against his firewalls and he smiled. That gravsled was exactly the woman he was waiting for. He let enough of his protocols down that she would know she'd hit her target.

The sled stopped and he knew her eyes had picked out his perch. The sled started again until she parked it some twenty metras away, where the ground was still relatively flat. She hopped off and landed hard, her knees bending to take the extra force of the high-gravity landing.

She walked carefully, precisely with the grace of a born spacer and the extra effort required of someone used to significantly less gravity than the weight of Lithos. But her lips curved in a soft smile and her eyes danced with excitement. The wind blew her short gold-red hair into a wild sexy tumble, as though she had spent hours romping among the sheets with a vigorous lover. Her skin was completely different from the last time he'd seen her, as it was different every time he'd seen her. Now it was a pale peach, reminiscent of ancient humanity and dotted with tiny patches of alluring specks of tan and brown. He wanted to find every last one of those specks, as he was suddenly certain that they covered her from head to toe. Galita Serhadze was nothing if not thorough.

The effects of the wind and the sun and her own apparent excitement tinged her cheeks with a pale pink the color of a fine rose quartz or a strawberry just beginning to blush from green-white to luscious, juicy red.

He was hard. Painfully, teeth-grittingly hard. He was grateful he'd worn the heavy canvas and synth-leather pants he used for climbing in the ravines. At least he might be able to stand up and keep some semblance of dignity.

"Thank you for coming, Ms. Serhadze." His voice sounded slightly hoarse and he hoped she wouldn't notice that either, having never truly met him before.

"Come on, Mardon, I think you can call me Galita, don't you think?" Her smile became lopsided and her eyes shuttered to guard her inner soul. "After all, if you bring a woman to her knees with an orgasm, you've earned the right to use her first name. Although I don't know." She folded her arms under her breasts and those twin mounds strained against the simple linen sleeveless shirt she wore. "Since you left me with only the barest hint of where to find you afterward, maybe we should stick to surnames, Senior Kaen." She gave him a bow, as an apprentice would to a master. But she couldn't keep her wry amusement from the tiny flick of her head or the shake of her shoulders.

He flinched in response. He'd almost forgotten she was so damn good. She must have hacked the personnel files for the Lithian Information Department—files he'd run the security codes for himself. And so she'd discovered his position as lead InfoEng on the planet—actually, in the whole sector. Infinity forbid that she actually knew he'd been one of her examiners on Mars. Though if she checked the travel files...

"And, it's quite amazing this is the first time I've seen you face-to-face, Mardon Kaen. At least in the flesh. We were on Mars at the same time."

Meckna *shit*.

"Of course, Mars has only what, ten times the population of Lithos—maybe twenty. Surely it's pretty amazing that you arrived home only a day after I arrived on Lithos. Even though it had taken me a full week to arrange transport to this obscure little system." She looked around, taking in the stunning view of ravines and peaks, tall gray-green girdle trees and gingerbrush all lit in the stunning oranges of the Lithian star. The trickle of water could be heard deep below, one of the few places liquid water ran freely on the planet. Risheva spoke a wild language rarely heard anymore in the civilized galaxy.

She wrinkled her brow and cocked her head, as though she'd heard something she couldn't quite understand. *Excellent.* She already heard the throbbing, even without his suggesting its existence. He knew he was right.

"Can you hear it?"

She straightened, swallowing guiltily. He knew the constant worry of the InfoEng, he would begin to be unable to tell fantasy from reality. He still felt it, after a century. Only now it was a real concern. "I hear it too. Many do, not just those with full implants." All InfoEngs and some other professionals had wireless Tessnet hookups implanted in their skulls, with direct access into the cranial nerves.

Her eyes pierced his for a moment, bright eyes so intelligent that he thought he would drown in the flash of her insight. She was one of the youngest InfoEngs in the past thousand years and as far as Mardon could tell, one of the best he'd ever seen.

When the DMTR incident had first happened, Mardon had been resistant, even angry, with Irav Tok for flouting thousands of years of tradition and risking the tranquility and magic of Lithos in order to make his little weedpelt lover happy. He still wasn't sure it was the best thing for Lithos in the long term but instead of feeling threatened by Galita Serhadze's vast capabilities, he was simply glad that now she would live out a Lithian lifespan, two or even three times as long as most humans in the rest of the galaxy. The rest of the DMTR's crew might be a bunch of *tralcs* and lackwits but the discovery of Galita had helped soften his opinions toward the ship and the damage that had been done to Lithos by Jov Myrna.

Well, Tok's little doctor playmate, Matrissa Prospera, actually seemed to be pretty bright as well, not to mention Irav suddenly seemed to have lost the stick lodged up his ass for the last century or so. And Mardon had never thought he'd see icy Ivani Gorl crack a natural smile but the hydrologist from DMTR, Garom Sesh actually seemed truly smitten with the bitch. Mardon had served on the Board of Directors of the HLL Conglomerate for only a decade but he had to admit the changes the crewmembers of DMTR were making to the staid and irritable members of the Board were very welcome.

The look on Galita's face was one of bemused curiosity and he suddenly realized he'd been quiet for a very long time. He'd been thinking, true. But he'd also been staring at the beautiful, ripe breasts teasing him by being level with his face as he sat on a boulder. Her arms were still clasped under them, as though offering them up for his delectation. If he leaned forward a couple of metras, he'd be able to capture a nipple in his teeth through the thin linen of her shirt. He could already see the hardening buds thrust against the soft fabric and though the wind was probably just making her cold and he was being a bastard by keeping her exposed outside, he wanted to think that those nipples were hard for him.

He shook himself, forcing his mind away from the simulation of her body he was already constructing in his mind. It had been years since he'd created a sex sim from a live woman! He felt like a juvenile barely able to keep from coming at the mere proximity of a female. Snorting in repressed laughter, his eyes moved upward to see her eyebrows arched in a mixture of amusement and pique that was rather adorable. He cleared his throat. "Shall we go down into the canyons?"

"Is that why you brought me here? To take me on a nature hike?" Her voice dripped sarcasm colored with the barest hint of petulance.

"I did not bring you here. I simply told you where I would be." She was such a pleasure to tease. He wondered if she was ticklish.

She glowered at him. He stood in a fluid motion, towering over her and enjoying watching her stare at his chest just as hard as he'd looked at her breasts. She swallowed and he grinned, "Shall we?"

She just nodded. He placed a hand on her elbow, to lead her toward the steep path down into the most accessible of the Risheva canyons. His thumb brushed against the satiny skin of the inside of her elbow and he could feel her shiver. "Cold?" he asked, though he hoped that wasn't the reason.

"No." Her voice was firm, definite. A rich alto that he wanted to hear caressing his name, or shouting in wordless pleasure. He edged in front of her and forced himself to let go of her arm, the memory of her skin making his fingertips tingle. Slowly they descended into Wyr Canyon, one of the closest to the entrance of the main Risheva mine. Pebbles rained down into the canyon as they walked along the aged path. He had to give Galita credit for doing her research — she'd worn decent shoes for the hike. The rich brown-red of the rock walls enveloped them, pulling them into Lithos' embrace the farther down they went.

Galita began to whistle, a startling sound that initially caused him to jump and stare at her but she shrugged her shoulders and kept right on whistling. A light, pretty tune, the music soon swirled with the rolling river and the wind and then ricocheted off the walls until it was a symphony. He inhaled the sweet air of his homeworld and wondered once again at the beauty of this place, still new to him after a century and a half of experience. As she let the song fade, he turned to look into Galita's face and saw the wonder in her face, tears sparkling in the corner of her eyes. Yes, she would manage to make Lithos even more beautiful.

Neither of them broke the echoing silence and they continued to walk. They reached the bottom of the canyon and the south entrance of the Risheva mine more than an hour after starting. The gaping entrance appeared suddenly within a large stand of trees, heavily laden with oblong fruit, the roaring river just ten metras away. It was a beautiful place, he'd always thought it an adventure to enter within the bowels of Lithos, something raw and real to counter the seduction of Tessnet diving. He hoped she'd feel the same.

Her eyes were huge as she looked into the dark. "This is the mine then?"

"Yes. More than eight thousand years old."

"And yet, not a drop of copper ore is ever shipped from Lithos. And it hasn't been for as long as I could find accurate records." Her eyes darted around the cavernous entrance, taking in every minute detail, from the beams made from native girdle trees to the glassy smooth floor that had been carved out millennia ago by prospectors with laser tools.

Damn, she was sharp. She did her research like a professional should—did he really think she'd come in here blind? A thrill ran through him when he realized that the potent combination of respect and desire he felt for her were leading him down strange mental pathways—pathways that ended not just with them fucking in every known position and inventing a couple of new ones but waking up in bed with her. Scenes of her walking through the hallways of his home, even a brief flash of her holding a red-haired infant whose skin flashed a matching brilliant red when it cried. He had to find a diversion for himself—and answer her statement in a coherent manner.

Not trusting himself to speak, he walked over to one of the tall trees nestled in the floor of the canyon. They were old friends and the fruit was a secret treat for those who made the journey to Risheva. He plucked one from a low branch and walked to Galita, who was looking at him once again as if she questioned his hold on sanity.

He held up his rough-skinned treasure. "This is a Lithian avocado." Reaching into the back pocket of his trousers, he flicked open a utility knife and sliced the fruit lengthwise, twisting with a practiced motion.

"I've had avocado…it's still a delicacy on Earth. But I've never seen the trees before."

He opened the fruit and revealed the bright blue-green flesh. She gasped and he smiled. "The Lithian avocado is a bit different. You've had Lithian pomegranates of course. Tried any other of the fruits that have gone feral here?" He made even slices into the flesh, peeling the rich fruit from the skin as she watched.

"I've had grapes that turned into jade, Rdani blackfruit that became onyx and some kind of vegetable from Eados that tasted bitter but I'm told ages into citrine. But I have to admit, I've never had non-simulated food that was quite so…blue."

He laughed. She had such a refreshing view of the world. "This is the only kind of copper we export anymore, I'm afraid. Turquoise is full of copper." He held a slice to her lips and with no hesitation she took a bite, revealing small, perfect teeth and a pink tongue that fed his fantasies. He popped a slice in his own mouth. It was good—almost buttery. But the taste of the rich flesh needed something more—and he imagined that the bead of sweat running down her neck after the long hike would be the perfect accent. The only thing more perfect would be the taste of the juices of her pussy. Ripe and salty sweet, the perfect complement to the lush metallic tang of Lithian avocado.

Watching her savor the flavor of the fruit—oh, that made him rock hard. Even the heavy trousers he wore weren't going to hide the bulge of his cock. Her eyes had fluttered closed but apparently they weren't completely shut, her red lashes dancing on her cheeks. A blush crept over those cheeks as he watched and he realized she knew exactly how much she was affecting him. When that pink tongue came out to claim the last bit of blue on her bottom lip, he groaned.

"Very tasty." She was looking at his crotch as she spoke, not at the remains of the fruit he still held in his hand. "Are we going inside anytime soon? I'd like to discover exactly why you'd track me down across half the galaxy to come to a hole in the ground—though the setting is lovely."

He reached for her hand and was surprised at how small it felt in his own. Small but not at all childlike, with long nimble fingers that threaded through his own on instinct. Tugging her forward, he walked into the darkness.

Ancient engineering was nothing to sneeze at and a series of dim amber lights flared to life the moment their heat signature was detected by automatic sensors. The hollow tunnel through which they walked grew more and more narrow, jutting out into multiple channels following the veins of copper that once ran through the rock. He shuddered at the thought of hacking them out, knowing what they were. Or at least, he suspected what they were, if he and the others weren't truly losing their minds.

"Why did they stop mining here? Did the supply run out?" Galita did not look afraid, only curious. He was glad she didn't seem to suffer claustrophobia, as it would make her task that much more difficult.

"No, there's more copper in this mine than in the rest of the quadrant put together. The miners stopped voluntarily. The crying was too much to handle."

"Crying?" The tone of her voice held no trace of disdain, only curiosity.

"It faded millennia ago, though the legends of haunting persisted. But I assure you, there is nothing here that is malevolent." *At least, there hasn't been anything aggressive to natives.*

She seemed to have a similar thought and swallowed audibly. She stepped a little closer to him, her thigh brushing against his and her elbow linking with his. He gritted his teeth and pushed down the instinct to spin her into the rough rock wall and kiss her until neither of them could breathe.

Just when he was about to succumb to his instinct to ravage, a thrumming of a completely different kind started. The soundless singing that was beautiful and terrifying all the same time, the same sirens' song that had convinced him and several dozen other Lithians that something was special about this mine. Possibly about the entire planet of Lithos.

"What is that?" Galita's voice was hushed, disbelieving. "It's... It's..."

"I don't know. We... I have suspicions but I've not been able to prove them. We need to go deeper to get the full effect."

He tugged at her elbow and she followed unresisting, relying on him to guide her through the winding tunnels as she was concentrating hard on the unique call of the caves. By now, there were no more lights installed and Mardon pulled a diode lantern out of his pocket and unfolded the thin shell which provided enough light to ease their passage into the deep warm darkness.

"There's blue here...in the walls..." she whispered, her lips close to his ear as he bent down in the increasingly narrow passage.

"Turquoise—a more raw form than the avocados but always present with the copper and shale."

The aged green patina was markedly different from the surrounding limestone and the blue peeking from beneath it was a dead giveaway. This was a vein of copper, exposed and waiting to be tapped. He was so used to not touching it directly that he didn't even think to warn her. But he couldn't bring up the words fast enough when she darted forward, a long nail scratching past the green and revealing the warm red-brown sheen of living copper.

When she screamed, he was prepared for the worst. But she didn't faint, or go catatonic. She smiled. A brilliant smile that seemed to light her up like a candle. He wouldn't have been surprised if her skin began to glow.

"Oh, it's beautiful." Her eyes were glazed, unfocused and seemed to take on a copper color. A wind arose in the tunnel and her wild red hair rose up in a cloud around her. He peeled off the layers of shields and firewalls blocking his implants and tried to see if he could reach her, make sure she wasn't trapped by the planet and the code that no one had been able to unravel.

But her shields were still intact. In fact, all her condition signals were online, in tiptop shape. Wherever she was, she was doing fine. He could only watch and wait, while she communed with Lithos in a way that many had tried before and no one had been able to accomplish. He should be jealous. He should be furious. But really all he could do was twiddle his thumbs and wait impatiently for the planet to be done with her so that he could get on with his planned seduction. If he didn't get his hands on that body soon he was going to explode and watching the expression of shocked pleasure on her face as she touched otherness for the first time—well, he wanted to be the one to put that look on her face, he wanted to see her eyes light up as he rammed his cock into her and he wanted to see those eyes as he made her see stars.

Mardon leaned against the wall, his eyes focused on her through half-closed lids and without his conscious will he constructed a sim in his head, half reality and half fantasy. Galita was awash in warm light in the garden of his home. Her clothes had been banished and he could finally see the ripe peaks of her nipples, pale and perfect as they drew tight with want. She was merely a step away, close enough for his naked cock to strain toward her body, seeking to bury itself home in her warm sheath.

Her arms wrapped around his neck and her breasts were crushed against his bare chest, his cock trapped against her stomach. His hands slid to cup her ass and his lips traced the edge of her jaw, tasting the sweet saltiness of her skin and inhaling the Rdanian honeysuckle fragrance of her hair. But before his hands could slide up her rib cage to cup the fullness of her breasts or ease around her hips to slip between her wet folds to tease her clit, she pulled away.

This was not part of a normal sim. The brilliant teasing smile that started with the slight upward tug of full rosy lips and came to life with the sparkle of amber brown eyes—that wasn't something a sim could ever fully capture. He was held in shock, realizing she had bypassed the minimal security he'd left up when he'd tried to check on her and now she was controlling this simulation.

Her nails raked down the muscles of his chest, leaving slight scratch marks that burned into his already scorching skin. He gripped her ass tightly, wanting to lift her up and onto his cock but she had a very different idea of what she wanted to do. She slipped out of his grasp, wiggling down, down, down—the tip of her sexy pink tongue barely touching his chest and then his stomach, as that smile continued to tempt him into insanity.

She was on her knees before him and his hands were buried in her hair before he had even realized it. One small hand wrapped around the thick base of his cock and he groaned in response. This was much, much better than any sim he'd ever experienced. Tessnet rendezvous were common enough but this was something more real, more vivid than he could ever remember. The silk of her hair between his fingers, the painful throb of his arousal as he waited for that naughty tongue to circle the head of his cock.

Instead, she darted right for the leaking drops of pre-cum, dipping into the slit to taste him. He pulled her hair with unconscious force and she caught the head of his cock in her teeth, reminding him exactly who was in charge. He loosened his grip and she finally ran that wicked tongue around his cock, stroking the glans with delicious pressure. Then she pulled him deeper, pushing him against the roof of her mouth increasing the wonderful friction until he thought he would explode. He knew he was leaking profusely, his balls high and tight and ready to come—but he didn't want to give up so easily. He wanted to be trapped in the hot heaven of Galita's mouth for an hour—a month—a year. The only thing he wanted more was to taste the juices of her folds and to hear her scream his name.

Just the thought of tasting her and he was again on the edge of losing control, thrusting into her mouth until he burst. She squirmed against him, her nipples brushing against his knees. He wondered if she had seen the image of his desires, how in his version of events, he would have her pinned against the wall, his long tongue inside her pressed against her G-spot, tasting her cream as he flicked his thumb against her clit and she shattered in his arms. At the same moment that image washed over him, she sucked him completely into her mouth, her hand cupping his balls firmly as she swallowed his head deep into her throat. He couldn't help gripping her hair and thrusting and he watched her eyes light up in triumph as he lost control. Her rosy lips wrapped completely around the thickness of his cock and the devilish look in her eyes was the last straw. He bellowed out a warning before erupting streams of semen into her hungry mouth.

She continued to suck as his knees grew weak, barely able to hold him up as his essence seemed to drain out of his cock and into her, like she was a beautiful succubus and he, her willing victim. When she finally released him he collapsed hard to his knees, pulling her lips to his and tasting his cum on her lips and tongue as he told her without words how incredible she was. He thought she must have drained every ounce of his need from him, so he was amazed at his voracious appetite, even in virtual reality, as his cock filled again with hot blood for her. Her breasts against his chest were too tempting and he pulled away from her drugging mouth to suck a nipple into his mouth, tasting the sweetness of her flesh and planning to sample every flavor she had to offer.

She gasped as his tongue touched the hard tip of her nipple and when he bit the sweet flesh she moaned so loudly he thought the tunnels must ring with the sound. Tunnels? What…weren't they in his garden a moment ago?

She wrenched away from him and with a flash the darkness crept in and reality filtered through his consciousness. His trousers were around his ankles as he knelt on the floor of the tunnel. Galita, her lips swollen and glossy with his semen, was backing away, her eyes wide with fear. Her shirt was in tatters but he had no memory of ripping it open to get to the beautiful breasts now exposed to his view.

Whatever had happened, it crossed the line between fantasy and reality, a big no-no for InfoEngs, or for anyone who dived for information on the Tessnet. It was critical to understand the boundaries of reality at all times. He'd never had this kind of lapse and he was terrified and awed at her power over him. Galita appeared equally frightened, almost like a lost little girl—or an innocent. The blush on her cheeks, her wide eyes. If she hadn't just given him the best damn blowjob of his life he'd have thought she was some virginal princess. Her mouth opened and closed as she searched for words. He already knew words would mean nothing. He didn't want to frighten her but he had to prove to her that what they were feeling was completely real. He crawled forward, intent on kissing her. He covered her body with his and watched the deep brown of her eyes grow soft in response. His cock throbbed against her bare stomach and the sweet smell of her arousal filled his nose along with the dust of the tunnels and the copper alive in the air. His lips ghosted over hers, like the wings of a starfly fluttering over a crystalline blossom that could shatter under too much pressure.

But it wasn't light enough. She rolled away, scrambling to her feet and running pell-mell back through the tunnels toward the entrance of the mines. It took him a full minute to realize what had happened. Fighting with his trousers he cursed at himself in ten standard galactic dialects. He was an idiot and a beast. He'd probably just chased away the only person capable of talking to Lithos, with the demands of his damn cock. Next time, he'd have to keep it in his pants, even in his fantasy world. But in the privacy of his bedroom, he knew she would figure prominently in his imagination for decades, if not for the rest of his long Lithian life.

He walked out with a purposeful stride. This time, he would go to her.

* * * * *

Interlude

Jov Myrna sat in his perfectly clean, optimally proportioned prison cell and sulked. He ignored the droning of the holovision playing its endlessly looping rehabilitation programs and contemplated his sorry state. Now Galactic Internee number 169AΣ7ϕ8*99, Jov's life was determined by a meticulously studied and regimented routine that the Galactic Corporate Attorneys had hashed out during centuries of suits and countersuits. Most of this time he spent trying to avoid the three Karogian pirates who'd ended up in the same detection facility on a barren moon of Eados VI.

He was sure that they would gladly wring his neck rather than allow him to testify against them. Even if they would instantly be mindwiped for violence within the prison. They were so damn insane, they probably would risk it just for the satisfaction of hearing his neck crunch. Shivering, he wondered how someone as bright and handsome as himself could have fallen into such straits. He was unappreciated and underpaid as a low-ranking officer on DMTR. The ship had been full of idiots like that little whore Matrissa Fucking Prospera, who'd been the one to ruin all his carefully constructed plans. He was certain she'd fucked enough of the pirates that they'd given her immunity like him and as soon as everyone else was down for the count she'd flown off to the richest planet in the quadrant and used her slick little cunt to acquire a big, fat sugar daddy who'd helped her take the ship that should have been his to save!

Somehow, instead of being a lauded hero, he'd gotten turned into a bad guy and heaped with the blame for every bad thing that had happened to DMTR. Hell, even his mother was barely talking to him. She'd only sent him a dozen of his favorite *usjal*-root cookies in her last care package. And she wouldn't tell him about why the hell the package had been shipped from thrice-damned Lithos. Why the fuck were the crew of DMTR on Lithos? What the motherfucking hell was so damn special about that slice of desert shithole? And why the goddamn hell did he face fifty years in this mind-numbing cell without a piece of female ass in a million leagues, just for dropping a little rain on the place?

He hoped that Juud and his crew were full of it. This cell was better than the alternative—banishment to the uncharted quadrant with nothing but the clothes on your back and a bone-deep tattoo declaring you couldn't work or trade anywhere on any civilized system. But he'd just had to shoot his mouth off to Juud and the other Qsakian Syndicate cronies. Tell them all about the secret weaponry on Lithos. Had to keep the guys entertained so they'd offer him a little protection from the fucking Karogians. So he'd exaggerated a little. He really didn't have a motherfucking clue how the Lithian had cured the plague. But talking about how he'd been overthrown by advanced counter-bioweapons made a great story. Better than saying he'd been duped by a fucking little cunt who he'd not even had the chance to taste.

Juud had said he'd come back for him, use some contacts to ease the way out through the "back door". Jov wasn't too thrilled with the idea but he didn't think Juud would let him live very long if he didn't come along when push came to shove. They wanted his astronavigation background to get them to Lithos. Jov would rather he'd never set eyes on the goddamn place again.

Juud had been out for three standard days. Maybe he'd forgotten—found some other con to work.

But when the lock buzzed open hours earlier than the precise schedule allowed, Jov knew that for the foreseeable future he was well and truly the Syndicate's bitch.

Fuck.

*****

The small ship hovered over the sunside of Lithos, disguised in the latest and best x-ray stealth shielding that laundered money could buy. Jov Myrna tried to huddle into himself and appear as small as possible, hoping that no one would try to ask him any more questions. He'd gotten them to the damn planet. Sure it had taken four tries and a burn across the back of his hands with a plasma pistol to get him to finally get the transdimensional math right but they were here, fuck it! He didn't know anything else.

He wished he did. They'd taken weeks to prep for this mission after cracking him out of prison. Now that he'd served his function, he knew that if they weren't so damn worried about being detected in orbit before they'd gotten their recognizance data, he was pretty sure they would chuck him out the airlock rather than waste the oxygen on him. These guys were serious criminals and they made the Karogian pirates look like petty pickpockets. And the Syndicate had decided that Lithos was a gurkplum ripe for the picking.

On the screen at the front of the bridge, a display of the planet's dull surface was flowing past as they made their orbit. They'd been at this for hours and Jov hadn't seen anything but deserts and tundra and the occasional mountain range. Nothing really passing for a large city and certainly nothing that would be a weapons facility. There were nasty looks coming his way and he was racking his brains trying to come up with a way to escape.

The viewscreen brought into focus something new for a change, some kind of lake or inland sea that stretched out on the edge of one of the deserts near the center of sunside. It sure was beautiful—hell it looked like some kind of giant pearl out here in space. Give some cunt a gem that big and you were guaranteed a hell of a lay!

The alarms started blaring, the lights flashing a dull red that signaled they'd been detected!

Veins of Turquoise

Juud Largos was screaming in rage at the viewscreen, while the pilot was hitting every damn button to get the dimensional thrusters online and get them out of orbit fast. "Motherfucking hell! I paid three million credits for this damn x-ray scanning system! They said it would be completely undetectable. What the fuck happened?"

Juud glared accusingly at the signals tech, who turned ash pale as a pistol was waved under his nose. "Sorry, sir. But that...the lake down there—it bounced the modulated x-ray scan back as a laser sir! Like a spotlight lighting up our position from the ground."

The Lithian system disappeared from the screen as they went hyperdrive. "Fucking asses, all of you! They have some seriously advanced tech and know how to disguise it that well and we haven't found out before now! I tell you, we are coming back and we are bringing half the damn Syndicate fleet. Lithos will either be the Syndicate's latest, greatest toy, or it will be a hunk of burned-out ash!"

Jov shivered. The man meant it. Every goddamn word. He had to get off this damn boat and disappear deep into the underbelly of the galaxy. He didn't want to see what was coming.

Chapter Three
Another dance?

She ran. Like a lermouse, Galita ran and cowered in her rented house, running from real life. Galita was angry and ashamed of herself. Running from the most fascinating thing she'd experienced in her lifetime, because the feel of a real man's tongue on her nipple and his hands cupping her ass all became too much to handle. She'd acted like a frightened little virgin.

She wasn't! Well, technically maybe she was. Galita had gotten her hymen pierced just like every other thirteen-year-old girl during her coming-of-age party. It had been neat and painless, the medical mech was top of the line. PTRA—the ship of her birth, always had everything top of the line. Everything had been just precisely perfect and that's probably exactly why she left.

So why had she run now? Back to the guesthouse that Irav Tok had found for her on short notice, with the taste of Mardon on her tongue and her knees quaking like a Terran jellyfish. The owner of the house and the estate was off on the other side of the galaxy at the moment, at least, that was what Matrissa had said. The servants, both sapiens and mechs, seemed pleased to have something to do. The estate seemed vast, with limitless skies a soft thin blue and the ever-present orange of the Lithian sun throbbing high in the sky. The twisted trees and carpets of hardy plants softened the hard edges of the landscape but the beauty of the wide-open space was still undeniably powerful. She gazed out the window into the cloudless sky and rubbed her temples.

Veins of Turquoise

The first thing Galita had done once Mardon had left her shaking on her knees in that hallway in Aroll, was to call Matrissa on the Tessnet. The video feed showed a very heavily pregnant Matrissa Prospera uncomfortably shifting as she smiled at Galita.

"Matrissa! Tell me again why you decided against a uterine replicator?" About half of Phytos women bucked the galactic trend and carried their children in their own bodies but that was on board ship, where lower gravity made things a whole lot easier.

"I didn't exactly know that Lithos symbiotes counteract contraceptive glands until I was too far along in the pregnancy to be able to transfer, even if I had wanted to!" Matrissa had laughed, her shoulder-length black hair bouncing across the lavender skin of her bare shoulders. How she could stand to be nude in the cold backwater she and Irav called home, Galita could not understand. The week she'd spent there when she'd first arrived, she thought her teeth would fall out from chattering every time she got out of her temperature controlled bedchamber. Although she'd appreciated Matrissa's efforts to ease her into life on Lithos, Galita had decamped to Aroll to establish her own life and routine reasonably quickly. There was always work for a good InfoEng and money wasn't a problem.

But she was still discontent. Searching for something that would calm the ache she held deep within her. Whispers on the edges of her mind drove her into the Tessnet, where she could find some peace but once again, not contentment. When Mardon Kaen had started watching her from afar, the whispers intensified and the longing resolved, to have a focus.

She could still taste the earthiness of him, the flavor of him that seemed embedded in her consciousness now. Simulation was good but now she understood how the feel and taste and smell of a man could never truly be replicated. She licked her lips, wanting to taste him again. It frightened her, that the barrier between fantasy and reality had slipped so much that she'd imagined she was wrapping her lips around his cock and it had actually happened!

And then there was Lithos. Always whispering on the edge of her consciousness, she now understood the soft caress in her mind she'd felt the moment she'd set foot planetside. Was this the siren song that every Lithian felt? The need that drew them back here from any far-flung destination in the known universe? She couldn't understand the words—the voice was too big, too alien for words. But desire and dreams were laden in every singing electron laced in those copper veins. She wanted, no, she needed, to know more. But she wasn't ready for it.

Her desire for Mardon had pulled her away from whatever lived in that mine, or perhaps his desire for her. She could taste how much he wanted her and with his firewalls down she was drawn into his mind and his fantasy before she could even question the ethics of it. She had to be there, had to soothe the ache she felt in him and in herself.

It had been like no sim she could remember. That's because it had been live and sim, fantasy and reality, all at the same time. The musky taste of him filling her mouth, the scent of him that lingered in her synapses, the feel of his firm thighs under her hands and the strange sense of dominance and submission all rolled together. She wanted to do it again and this time she wanted to feel that huge cock inside her. She couldn't fit all of him in her mouth and she was sure that fitting him inside the confines of her sheath would be painful—but she had a feeling the pain would be worth it, would just make it all that much more real. The awkwardness, the fear, the idea that she could make a mistake, all of that was part of the dangerous allure of the act.

She had to get it out of her system! She had to get her senses back under control before she lost her grip on reality, just when she was being tested the most. Whatever was in that copper mine, was unlike anything she'd ever felt. It was raw emotion, raw desire but needs and desires so different from her own she couldn't make sense of anything, only the vibrant perception of otherness—and the sense that it was not at all evil. In fact, in touching those veins, she had felt embraced, more at home and cared for than she'd ever felt in her life.

Either that, or there was some serious, unregistered hallucinogenic properties in those avocados and her warning sensors hadn't caught the biological signature of a drug.

She rolled her eyes and flung herself back on the bed, staring at the soft curve of the ceiling. The guesthouse was adobe, sculpted from clay made from the local rock. There wasn't a straight wall, everything seemed organic, comfortable and natural. The mech housekeeper had provided a history of the place. How long ago the ancestors of the current owner had created this home by hand—a pet project that became a labor of love. The main home, less than a kilometra away, had been created in a similar fashion, made out of the land rather than manufactured with artificial tools and textures of advanced technology.

What did she want?

The answer echoed back to her in the cacophony of her mind.

Mardon.

Whatever challenges she would find on this planet, whatever wonders awaited her back in that mine, Galita knew she would not be able to listen unless she fulfilled her own desire and satisfied the craving clouding her mind. Lithos wanted her to be happy—and without knowing how it felt to have Mardon slide hot and hard within her, Galita would always be wondering and never be content.

Shooting up from the bed, she was suddenly determined to have what her body was screaming for. Pressing a button to change a wall display to show a digital mirror, Galita ran through a series of possible skin tones and patterns meant to make herself as alluring as possible. Blue? Interesting but it didn't feel right. Purple, as always, clashed horribly with the bright red of her hair, both on her head and the trimmed hair of her sex. Vertical stripes? A bull's-eye target on her stomach and thighs, centered on her clit?

She threw back her head and laughed at herself—she hadn't been this nervous in years. She'd always been sexually dominant in sims, never felt so worried about the way she looked when it was something she could change so easily. Hell, in sims she could make her hair deep midnight blue or white blond or a tiger stripe of both if she felt like it!

In reality, she had to worry if her clothes, which she always chose for comfort, were sexy enough or if her hips were too wide or why her parents had managed to gift her with such horribly colored hair with a mind of its own!

In a sudden burst of inspiration, Galita bit her lip and watched the slow progress of her idea take form on the palate of her skin. Copper-colored lace wove across the pale peach of her skin, forming an intricate pattern that fooled the eyes into thinking she wore a skintight body suit, popular in certain parts of the galaxy. The lace weaved over her mound and covered her nipples convincingly but she was deliciously, daringly exposed.

Now, suitably attired for seduction, she had to find her target. Diving into the trancelike state for a Tessnet search, Galita looked for information on Mardon Kaen, InfoEng. Lithos had a fine transportation system—he could truly live anywhere within the habitable zone, from the hot tropics near that new lake that Garom Sesh was investigating, to the cold tundra of Matrissa's new home. With information swirling around her, it felt cleansing to dive into the endless streams of data—a comfortable coming home to her native environment. The hunt for information was her fascination and her best skill and she relished the challenge. Surprisingly, this particular challenge ended much closer than she could have guessed. She laughed at herself once again, wondering how she had never heard the name of the owner of this marvelous guesthouse. She even suspected Irav and Matrissa of matchmaking.

Veins of Turquoise

The owner was not on the other side of the galaxy at the moment. Mardon Kaen was on the same estate, a kilometra away. And, given the disturbances in her personal access records, he was probably hunting for her as well. The air outside was warm enough she didn't even need a covering if she felt daring enough to go naked—and she most certainly did. Leaving the house and walking to the gravsled parked outside, she felt the Lithian wind over her naked flesh and shivered with excitement and nerves. Powering up the sled, she coasted over the living desert and toward the man who made her blood sing. If he was going to rock her world, she would do her damnedest to rock his.

* * * * *

Molded out of the red desert, the clean lines of the house fitted with everything she'd discovered about Mardon—big and red but somehow still subtle. The wide windows were dark from the outside but she was sure from the inside they must offer a sweeping view of the rock and rugged plants that made the Lithian countryside strangely compelling. She raised a hand to knock on the solid front door, only to practically stumble when the door slid aside as though it already recognized her.

The only sound she could hear upon walking into the front foyer was the sigh of the wind and the distant trickle of water. There were no human servants and only a silent mech that watched her with black, expressionless sensors as it indicated a direction for her to walk in search of the master of the house. Thick rugs warmed the flagstone floors and comfortable sofas and low tables collected in groups around a real fireplace. The home was simple and warm but still echoed with emptiness. If Mardon was here—he was alone. That made her sad and she wasn't sure why.

It was more than how she had decided to fuck him in the physical sense rather than the virtual one. She wanted to be there afterward, be held in his arms and find out how he looked when he slept. Where was this coming from? What did she know about this man? That he'd found something extraordinary about Lithos and he'd decided, for some mysterious reason, to share it with her—a young InfoEng from the ship that had almost destroyed his homeworld. Why did he trust her?

Had he pulled strings with the Information Department's headquarters on Mars to access her records? Had he observed one of her psych tests? Galita almost shivered at the sense of invasion. She'd bared everything in those tests—she'd had to. If Mardon had seen those, experienced her own internal mindscape—could he still trust her? Want her?

She was certain he wanted her. It had been a pretty vivid fantasy sim she'd hacked into and his picture of her had been pretty accurate—no hugely inflated breasts or falsely perfect features. He'd even known the scent of her shampoo.

The water was what called to her—the only sound that seemed different, not out of place but noticeable in the quiet solitude of the house. The musical trickle led her out of wide crylic door out on to a garden terrace. Whatever outsiders would say about Lithos being barren, Lithians looked on their gardens with pride and passion and Mardon was no exception. Flowers in a dozen colors, ripe fruit ready to be plucked or allowed to age into the finest gems. Foliage in interesting shades of gray and blue and pale green. The water was a subtle fountain, a natural-looking cascade of rocks and shalemoss, surrounded by low stone benches. Views of the wide-open countryside and the distant canyons beckoned one to sit and stare in quiet contemplation.

Galita only had eyes for Mardon. The red-brown of his skin melded with the deep colors of the landscape, until it seemed like he had been carved from the rocks of Lithos. She'd heard rumors about men made of clay but too much vitality pumped through Mardon's veins for him to be anything but very much a human male. He was sitting on one of the stone benches, lost in a data trance, something she could easily recognize and she hoped she wasn't disturbing him at work. Normally, an InfoEng's proximity alarms would alert one to the approach of a stranger but whatever he was doing, he was so absorbed that he disregarded the warnings. She waited quietly, appreciating the view of him. He'd stripped off his shirt since that morning and his chest was every bit as impressive as she could have hoped. The dark brown peaks of his nipples rode on the sculpted chest of a man who climbed the walls of the ravines every chance he could. He'd exchanged the dusty trousers she'd pushed down to his ankles in the mines for a pair of loose Ralian silk pants, a common sight on Lithian men everywhere she'd been. Comfort here was a priority.

A drop of water snaked down the line of his neck from his damp hair, which was a shade darker from being wet. She wet her dry lips. She needed that drop of water. That exact drop of water on her tongue. Nothing else would do.

Imagining him in the shower was not helping her make a calm, reasoned explanation of her decision. Imagining being with him in the shower, having water cascade over her as he held her hips tight and pounded her into a wall—she blew out a breath.

That small action seemed to break him out of his Tessnet trance and his eyes focused on her instantly. Suddenly being the object of such a man's intense focus was startlingly powerful. If Galita thought she'd been aroused before, it was nothing to the fire burning in her now. His eyes, as blue as that luscious turquoise fruit they'd shared, traversed her from nose to toes and she tingled everywhere as though his fingers had flickered over her skin.

"So, you were here under my nose the entire time?" His voice seemed more amused than angry and she breathed a sigh of relief.

"Only for the last few minutes." She was glad she'd changed her skin tone, for the complex lacey pattern concealed her blushes much better than the pale peach she'd worn earlier. "I was enjoying the view." He could take that any which way he wanted.

"You are staying in my guesthouse. You've been there for a day…and a night…and I didn't even know it."

She pursed her lips and felt her back stiffen in defense. "Is this a problem? Irav and Matrissa said that the owner of the estate was away. Shall I leave?"

He stood up and strode forward, standing so close her nipples tightened to painful points, making it obvious that the pattern she wore was only skin deep—only an alluring concealment of her naked skin.

"The only problem is that I could have been doing this much, much sooner." He bent and the feel of his lips on hers made her head spin but his huge hands cupping her naked breasts made her groan. They needed to talk. They needed to settle a thousand things, she needed to understand exactly what he expected from her. But what she wanted was exactly this, his hands and lips all over her.

Normally capable of multiple threads of thought and maintaining a dozen complex data streams, Galita couldn't bring up the knowledge of her own name, much less a coherent sentence. He pinched her nipples between thumb and forefinger and she bit his lip hard in response. He laughed and nipped her lip in return. Shaken out of her frozen state, her hands thrust into that wonderful wet red hair and deepened the kiss, trying to taste the raw thrill of a real, live kiss. There was no way he could know he was her first but she had a feeling he would be the best for a long, long time.

But he was too damn tall! She was tall for a Phytos but this was ridiculous. He was bent half over to kiss her and she wanted to feel him closer to her. She wanted more than the feel of those rough hands on her breasts, she needed to feel his lips and tongue and teeth on her nipples again. The first time in the mines, the sensations had been so shockingly good they had jarred her out of her Tessnet trance to realize that they were practically attacking each other in real life.

Now, fully awake and aware, she craved him—all of him. Not stopping to consider gravity and trusting those rippling muscles to be every bit as useful as they were impressive, she dug her fingers into his powerful shoulders and curled one leg around his thigh. He was hot enough to burn through those silk pants where his cock was rock hard and thrusting out to find her.

He responded to her actions instantly, sliding his hands away from their worship of her breasts, over her ribs and hips and finally cupping the bare curves of her ass, pulling her against his cock and making her let out a tiny scream of pleasurable shock. How else could she respond but to hop up and wrap her other legs around his hips? He bore her weight without the slightest flinch and as though he could read her mind he bent his head to suck a coppery nipple into his mouth. She threw her head back and stared through half-closed eyes in mindless wonder at the waltz of the Lithian moons. She was uncertain if the lights in the sky were real or a side effect of the lightning shooting through her. She couldn't know how the illusion of lace across her skin rippled and danced with her pleasure but Mardon certainly appreciated the view.

Her legs were wide open as she hung suspended in his arms and her engorged clit rubbed against his erection giving her flashes of raw delicious sensation. Did she want more, or did she want to escape? Run away instead of risking disappointment—run away before she would never be satisfied again by anything else.

He growled as though in response to her instinct to run, clutching her ass tightly and forcing her clit against his cock with enough force to send comets zinging across her field of vision. There was no way in Infinity that he was going to let her go without fucking her within a cetar of her life. With that knowledge, her inhibitions melted and all she wanted was to finally feel his cock slide within her.

Silk felt very interesting against her pussy but truly the pants had to go. She let go of one shoulder and smoothed her hand over the skin of his chest, promising herself she could come back to play with those tempting nipples later. But her goal was soon reached and she was tugging on that waistband and cursing the restrictions of physics and reality. She wanted those off five minutes ago.

He nipped at her nipple and she gave a tiny scream and he rose up to stare at her with those amazing blue-green eyes. With a firm yank at the waistband of those trousers, she made her wishes more than clear but was no closer to her goal, not with her legs wrapped around him and his cock practically holding the fabric up like a flag.

He pulled away from her, holding her in his arms with ease and she reacted instantly, reaching into those pants to pull out her treasure. He felt huge in her hand and she could feel the blood pulsing through him, shockingly real and alive. She brought him to the opening of her sheath and circled her hips, desperate to feel him inside her. He pulled on her hips, as desperate as she but as she began to sink down on to the thick throbbing cock she flinched, the stretching more painful than she had prepared herself for.

Mardon stopped cold, with willpower that seemed superhuman.

"You are tight," he whispered through gritted teeth. "Too damn tight. When was the last time…"

She drew in a worried breath, wondering if her inexperience would rob her of his respect. He stared into her eyes like he was trying to read her innermost thoughts and she forced herself not to try to check her firewalls for integrity, not that she could have come up with the brainpower for such an endeavor at the moment.

She moaned in defeat as he pulled away from her. He leaned back and splayed a hand across her back, moving a hand between them to circle a long finger around her clit and then thrust it deep within her. Galita yelped in surprise, loving the feeling and knowing that his cock would feel even better. But she was still slightly dry and very tight. This was very different from any sim sensations.

"Infinity—this is not going to work." Grunting hard, he pulled her firmly to his chest and his cock teased the lips of her pussy as he began a slow ungainly shuffle into the central home of the house behind them. His pants were around his knees and he tried to hop to get them off a few times, which caused Galita to giggle and hold on for dear life.

"Are we stopping?" she finally got up the nerve to ask.

He stopped dead, a look of agony crossing his features for a moment before they settled back into a mask of control. "Do you want to stop?"

In answer she let go of her iron grip on his shoulders and gripped his head, pulling him in for a kiss that made his cock throb against her folds. She wiggled in response and the shuffling walk turned into a comical hopping run. When he tossed her down on to a broad couch and fell on top of her, she gasped—first in surprise from the fall and then again at the shock of his naked body on top of hers, pressing her into the luxurious brown vardenpelt covering the sofa.

He hovered over her on his elbows. "You are full of surprises, Galita Serhadze. I don't know whether you are the most experienced, capable woman I've ever met, or the most innocent sex-kitten I've ever had the pleasure to initiate." He cocked his head at her, running his fingers lightly over the outer curve of her breast and causing her phytodermis to ripple in response. "What do you want to be?"

She couldn't force a complicated answer through her brain or past her lips. Nothing wry or sardonic or witty. Simply, "Yours."

His bright blue eyes flickered then with something unreadable but he lowered his face to kiss her lips with raw fire. His tongue licked at hers like a flame and he ground his cock against her swollen labia with a sinuous rhythm to match.

She did feel like she was going to burn to a cinder if he didn't come to the point and thrust that length of glorious cock into her. Her hand reached between them, determined to guide him to the place where she needed to feel him.

"No, no…not yet my scorching little goddess." He moved down to flick a long tongue over the aching tip of her breast. "It's been too long and I need to treat you right—and I need you too damn much to do that if you try to help."

Then he pressed her down into the lush fabric with hot, open-mouthed kisses on the underside of her breasts, her navel and her lower abdomen. His hands pulled her thighs apart and she arched her hips, hoping that this felt as good in reality as it had felt in sims.

With the first stroke of his tongue on her clit, she knew that the sims had lied. This was much, much better. Virtual reality experts and neurobiologists may claim that they can replicate every sensation known to mankind but they were wrong. The sims had been water and this was the finest wine. She was completely intoxicated.

Her hands dived into the thick red of his hair, begging him with words she couldn't form. Her lips were too busy moaning. She thought she understood arousal but the light circles around her clit, combined with sudden intense suction were making her wetter than she could ever remember being. She was sure that she would soak the incredibly expensive furniture she was splayed out upon but she didn't care and she didn't think Mardon did either. In fact, she swore she could feel his smile even as he worked his tongue over her inner lips and eased that long, thick finger into her sheath.

Her hips jerked and she screamed, closer than she could have believed to orgasm. A second finger joined the first and he pressed high and hard within her. The G-spot was not something mythical made up by programmers. The proof exploded behind her eyes as she shook beneath him, every muscle rigid with her climax.

Mardon continued to lap up her juices but let her down slowly as she melted into the couch. When he finally looked up at her, his eyes shone with smug satisfaction and his lips glistened with her essence. His fingers remained embedded inside her, moving slightly every so often just to drive her slowly insane with the aftershocks of pleasure.

"Now, my sweet kaleidoscopic treasure, now you are ready for me."

She blushed but since her skin was radiating a psychedelic display of muted colors, there was only the flush of heat to reveal her embarrassment. But there was such warmth in his eyes, so much desire, that soon the only thing she wanted was for him to stop teasing her and give her the main course, to satisfy her hunger for his cock.

He was finally in a mood to oblige. Mardon reared up on to his knees. From her position staring up at him he towered above her—and that cock looked huge! Would the thing even fit inside her?

Pushing aside that glimmer of fear, she scooted closer to him, planting her feet wide apart on the cushions supporting them and tilting her hips in invitation. His thumbs settled on her hipbones and his fingers dug into her ass he pulled her high against his thighs. His rigid cock pressed through her folds with infinite slowness and she was urgently impatient and anxiously grateful all at the same time. With sudden clarity, she realized the hands holding her so tightly were shaking with the effort of not slamming into her. He was not the one with all the control.

"Inside! Now, Mardon Kaen! Fuck gentleness, I need you now!" She could barely recognize her own voice but the effect it had on him was extraordinary. His eyes seemed to catch fire and glow such an intense blue she gasped. He thrust forward, encasing himself deeply within her and she cried out with the exquisite pain of it. It did hurt but only slightly—a stretching of muscles that had only been used in theory, never in practice. But being filled so completely was more than worth the ache.

"Fuck…did I hurt you? Oh, Infinity's ass…you are so tight." His beautiful eyes were clenched shut and he seemed to be fighting demons as a paroxysm passed over his face. He held himself completely still, long past the point when she needed time to adjust. She wanted it all. She wanted their bodies to slide together. She wanted to try every position ever invented on the Hyvan Pleasure Moon. She wrapped her legs around his waist and circled her hips, moaning at the slide of him within her.

His eyes popped open and he growled at her, his voice only increasing her need. "Woman! Give me a moment or you are not going to get the ride you deserve!"

"You can impress me with your suave skills later, big boy. Just fuck me this time. It's what we both want."

He arched one brown-red eyebrow and gave her a lopsided smile. "You asked for it."

He hiked her ass up even higher and pulled her hips against his until he was embedded so deep within her he hit her womb. Then he pulled out, almost all the way leaving her empty and frantic. He thrust back in quickly though and she relaxed in relief. He wasn't going to make her wait. He was going to make her very, very happy.

Galita wasn't relaxed for long. Soon she was panting, desperate, clinging to the powerful arms holding her hips and straining to meet each powerful thrust. It was raw, it was almost painful as her pussy stretched to accommodate the size of his cock. But it was so damn pleasurable that pain seemed only a distant small memory. The pulsing rhythmic slide of their flesh, the pants and groans and swearing to the gods of a dozen worlds, all of it was familiar from the sims and yet magnified so much as to be completely new.

The lightning singing in her blood was extraordinary though. He stared down at her with those incredibly intense eyes as though he was fighting a battle, with her and with himself. He was going to bring her to another orgasm if it killed him. A noble goal but she couldn't help the instinct to see him break and lose that control, to see him as vulnerable and animalistic as she felt.

She wasn't innocent. Not by a long shot. She'd probably had hundreds of different partners, even if it was in sims. And the skills she'd learned were not completely lost in translation. Clenching the muscles of her sheath hard, his rhythm was broken and he stopped, wrapped completely within her, his eyes shut tight and his grimace almost frightening.

You don't scare me, Mardon Kaen. She fluttered her muscles in patterns she'd developed through her copious experience and those blue eyes popped open once again, his full lips parted with shocked bliss.

"Oh, holy Mrdak and Yepp9n%$ttt..." She would have complimented him on his excellent pronunciation of Rdinian but he was intent on unwrapping her legs from their death grip on his waist and holding them up to his chest, her feet on either side of his ears. His hands caressed her calves and he swallowed audibly. She was equal parts irritated by her inability to break him and awed by the gentleness and care he treated her with.

Then he locked his arms around her thighs and began to use his whole body to thrust into her, her tight pussy made even tighter by the position of her legs. Her clit was pinched, smashed in the most amazingly wonderful way with every stroke and before she could comprehend the storm running through her, her legs were shaking, her hands desperately grabbing for something to keep her from flying off into the stratosphere.

He came with a shout, pumping into her with hot spurts of cum. Yelling in triumph Galita shuddered with her own brilliant explosion, gasping as Mardon fell forward, almost crushing her with his bulk. At the last moment he caught himself on his elbows but as she struggled to find her breath from the pleasure still spiraling through her in waves and eddies, she thought that she just might like being pinned beneath him. His cock was still locked within her as she was bent double, her legs trapped between them. He pulled away from her slightly, letting her slide her legs wider until she could slip them once again around to his back, pulling him snug against her so she could enjoy every last aftershock running through both of them.

Just at the moment when his weight would have become uncomfortable, Mardon expertly shifted them so that they were on their sides and he was still half hard inside her. The scent of his sweaty skin, the heat of his breath on her forehead, the slick skin of his chest against her cheek—all of it was glorious and new. Her satisfaction was bone deep and so was her exhaustion. A side effect of intense pleasure and intense exertion that had never been a problem when everything had been wrapped up in her cerebellum. Before she realized her peril, she was asleep, wrapped in the arms of a man who was still, essentially, a mysterious stranger.

Chapter Four
Rock and Roll

ଞ

Mardon didn't want to sleep. It was much more interesting watching Galita's face as she slept. How her slow rhythmic breathing sent a few strands of her too-short hair tickling her nose. He wondered if he could convince her to grow it. It was the most glorious red he'd ever seen and imagining it long and silky and wrapped around her like a cloak was making him swell inside her once again.

She moaned in her sleep as he slipped out of her, for the sake of her newly stretched, abused pussy. He was certain that it had been a long, long time since she'd had sex but the gods of half the galaxy could attest that she had remarkable skills. He couldn't wait to bury himself inside her again, to taste her sweet juice and nibble the peaks of her nipples. Her skin was the most amazing consistency, soft and yet alive, more reactive than any other woman he'd been with, and the colors, the colors made him want to coax pleasure from her again and again, just to see the dazzling display of rich swirling tones across her flesh. She would never, ever be able to hide her reactions to him.

Each breath made her beautiful tits rise and fall. They fit perfectly in his hands and her nipples were so sweet they were addictive. At the moment, the sweat-slick skin glistened in the soft orange light flooding the room and an abstract garden of light blue and blush pink, soft yellow and cool greens blossomed over the luscious mounds. Each nipple was like a ripe juicy berry, one dark pink, the other a plump purple. He couldn't restrain the urge to bend and give the purple one a soft lick and then watch it tighten into a bud the perfect size and shape for a frikberry from Hyvan III, one of the most delectable fruits known to man and an aphrodisiac to boot.

His slick cock submitted a complaint as another wave of raw need flooded through him. He'd just fucked her fast and hard, so deep he felt consumed. He should be sated and content but he only wanted more. He wasn't sure he'd ever get enough of her. Soon enough his own breathing became even and though he didn't fall asleep, he fell into a state of trance. Not a Tessnet trance, he had no desire to dive for anything when he held such a woman in his arms, but a trance of contemplation. He had never felt so close to another human being. He was always happy being an InfoEng, always at a distance from others, always considering the essence of reality with an objective eye. When he'd first felt the thrums of the mine, the voice of Lithos, everything he'd ever thought about the world and himself seemed slowly torn away. He'd had to question his sanity, the meaning of his life and he had begun to feel profoundly lonely.

The first time he'd set eyes on Galita Serhadze on Mars, the loneliness had gone. He hadn't even understood what was different, the lust roaring through him was screaming too loudly for him to break down the one-way mirror between them and spread her out on the crylic table and make her scream. His imagination had not come close to the reality of her taste, her scent, the feel of her pussy convulsing around his cock. Now, he wasn't sure he could give her up. If this was just a lustful fling, a reaction to the prevalent power present in the mines, if she was ready to wake up and walk away from him without looking back, he worried his soul would simply close down and he'd lose himself.

Being so vulnerable left a bad taste in his mouth. He opened his eyes and stared as her long lashes rested against the smudged peach of her cheeks. Nuzzling her temple, he bent to run his tongue over the shell of her ear—a much better flavor. She smiled and moaned slightly, moving closer to him and tightening her grip around his waist. Well, her subconscious certainly didn't want to run from him.

She didn't do this kind of thing often, her incredibly tight pussy was testament to that. A snarling beast of jealousy roared in his chest with the stray thought that another man would have the chance to see how beautiful she was when she was sleeping off the exhaustion of some really, really good orgasms. His ears were still ringing from her screams of pleasure. Who could blame him for feeling smug?

Those huge brown eyes fluttered open and stared straight into his. There was not a moment of confusion, just a wide smile that lit up her whole face. His brain knew it was too soon to expect her to want to do anything else, to fulfill her promise of "later". But his cock throbbed against her thigh and her honest smile of happiness rapidly turned sly and knowing. When she bit her full lower lip and her eyebrows arched in challenge, he crushed her breasts against his chest and claimed her lips again.

She kissed him back with a sleepy fervor, getting more and more passionate as she awoke fully. Her hands clutched at his ass and her legs parted so that his cock was slipping through the wet lips of her pussy. But he ignored the persistent screaming of his cock to ram back into that welcoming warmth.

He did let his fingers draw back and forth through the sticky wetness and she mewed in contentment, pushing against him and beckoning those fingers to come inside. He humored her and luxuriated in the satisfied grin on her face as two and then three fingers filled her sheath. Galita hiked her leg higher and higher, showing acrobatic prowess that he would definitely like to explore. Completely open to him now, she whimpered in response to his thumb passing over her clit. Her nails digging into his chest and likely leaving marks, she purred at him like a beautiful multicolored calico cat.

"Fuck me again, Mardon. Now."

He clicked his tongue at her, liking the swearing and liking the resulting blush at his censure even more. He bent over her, his teeth nipped at the lobe of her ear before growling, "This time, I get to choose when and how, my little kitten."

She blew out a breath, part pant of pleasure and part snort of derision. Then she arched her back, displaying her beautiful breasts, which before his eyes became luscious peach globes tipped in dusky pink, looking good enough to eat.

He grunted as his cock throbbed and his mouth salivated. "Oh, you play dirty, tigress."

She grinned at him and went so far as to wink. He pressed up against her G-spot in vengeance and her eyes practically rolled back in her head. She moaned loudly and began to shake but just before she would come gushing around his fingers, he withdrew, leaving her aching.

"Ah, Infinity's tits, you are cruel!" she yelped at him, panting hard and writhing to try to reclaim the wonderful pressure of his fingers on that spongy spot that he'd zeroed in on.

Having her at his mercy was certainly enjoyable but his cock, so recently satisfied, was demanding satisfaction once again. That and the pouting lips and sad eyes on Galita's face were arrows in the armor of his conviction to tease her.

"Fine! Fine! If you want to play that way, then I'd better do my best to disarm you." Lucky thing that the vardenpelt sofa was so wide, because he yanked at her hips to turn her over with enough force to send both of them crashing to the floor otherwise. Instead of having to coax her ass up into the air, she caught on as quick as lightning and was on her hands and knees, her ass thrusting up into the sky and her swollen pussy on glorious display, before he could try to form a command.

His cock did his thinking for him and he slid into her, his hands clutching her hips. She was throbbing around him, so tight he could feel her heartbeat in his cock and he was so sensitive he thought he'd explode from the slick heat that engulfed him in an inferno.

She'd been holding her breath and once he was embedded completely she took in a great gasp of air and moaned in pure happiness. The power he felt at being able to create such honest ecstasy was completely intoxicating. Her reactions were so real, so candid, that they blew the memory of every other partner out of his mind.

"Fuck, you are gorgeous." The trite words that dribbled from his lips couldn't explain the depth of his emotion, his need to explain how much he needed her.

She looked back over her shoulder at him with a saucy grin. Her eyes were glazed in pleasure and she pressed backward, forcing him deeper within her sheath. "I bet you say that to all the girls."

Damn it, she's never going to understand. It's her. Only her. His cock spoke better than he did and he snapped his hips back and rammed into her again, bending forward to capture her lips for just a moment before drawing back upright. He began to set a slow, deep rhythm, making sure to find exactly the right angle to feel her muscles pulse around him, her pussy trying to grab him and keep him. She felt like satin and his mind ceased to function when the blood in his body filled his cock to bursting.

The pace began to get faster, though he couldn't remember willing it to happen. He wasn't sure who the hell was in command but Galita's desperate whimpers began to register. Suddenly he felt her convulse, screaming, "Mardon!" at the top of her lungs as her thighs shook from the force of her orgasm. He was going cross-eyed trying not to follow her and losing the battle until an unexpected ally intervened.

The wall screen behind the couch flickered into full color, holographic life and Mardon stopped his thrusts and stared in dumbstruck rage at the giant image of Irav Tok filling the screen. Galita shrieked and she flung herself down onto the sofa cushion and her skin flickered into a deep midnight blue from her shoulders to her thighs. Mardon figured it was some kind of fear reaction, all her color cells going off at once. She let out a sound that sounded like, "Eep!" and tried to scoot away from him. Mardon gripped her hips and held her tight to him, his cock balls-deep in her.

"Did I call at a bad time, Mardon?"

Mardon wanted nothing more than to wipe that grin off Irav's face. But more than that, he wanted Irav's giant black head out of his living room so he could get on with the fuck of his life!

Mardon growled out in a voice an octave lower than normal, "What the fuck do you want, you ass?"

"No thanks, I've got my own Phytos to fuck. I'll pass." Irav flinched and there were simultaneous screeches as both Galita and Matrissa reacted to Irav's pathetic attempt at humor. The man never did have the ability to make a decent joke.

Galita tried to pull away again and once again Mardon kept her tight to his hips, his cock pulsing within her impatiently. She grumbled and just threw her hands over her head, doing her best to hide her blushing cheeks. Mardon restrained himself from laughing at her discomfort, as he was not at all in the mood. "Irav, I promise you I will have revenge. But with your priggish history, I doubt you called to spy on my sex life. So, what the fuck do you want?"

Irav managed to suppress his hilarity to look serious for a moment. "We've had some reports from Ivani at the Silith listening station. It looks like there's a fleet passing Lithos XI and coming into the system on full stealth mode."

"Fuck." Mardon slapped his hand down on the nearest surface, which was Galita's beautiful ass. She yelped and shivered slightly and his cock pulsed again as her pussy clenched at him. *Hmm…something else to explore later.* "So, they are coming then. Are the lawyers ready?"

"They've already beamed all the info to the GCA but you know it will take them at least a week to act. We're already clearing out Aroll and the population centers in case of bombardment attack. The atmospheric shielding is online, with the uninterruptible power we put in after that pissant Jov's stunt with the cloud cover. That played fucking havoc with the power systems for weeks."

"But it's not enough." Mardon spoke quietly but the silence following was deafening. He eased his grip on Galita, thinking she would pull away but she pushed closer to him, keeping his cock seated within her even as his blood rapidly returned to his brain.

She pushed backward harder and he sat on his heels as she fell into his lap, her hands coming up to cover her dark breasts. The blush still bright on her cheeks, she stared right at Irav as she spoke. "The Qsakian Syndicate?"

Irav nodded gravely and Mardon could feel as Galita relaxed into Tessnet trance. He wrapped an arm around her waist to keep her upright but in only moments she was back with a grimace marring her sweet face. He stroked his hand over her stomach and she jumped slightly, tipping her head back with a soft wistful smile before turning to Irav. "Five Cruisers and fifteen Darts are on the way. No Supercruisers, thank Infinity." Her lips gave a wry twist, "Glad I did all that practice hacking into their system a few weeks back."

Mardon bent to kiss the nape of her neck. She impressed the hell out of him and he'd been hacking systems far longer than she had. He'd simply assumed Qsakian security would be too damn good. Never assume.

He nibbled her ear, inhaling her scent—their combined scent—and his cock throbbed to life within her once again. She mewed in response, clenching her pussy against him and he gritted his teeth to prevent instantaneous explosion.

Irav's deep voice yanked them back to the problems bearing down on the planet. "Stealth mode is going to slow them down. It's likely we'll not see them for a good twenty standard hours."

"That'll let us clear the cities. Get a couple of ships started out of the system with children and caretakers. And give the lawyers more time to try to pull some strings at the GCA." Mardon sounded more hopeful than he felt.

Galita snorted. "Dream on. The Syndicate has more department heads on their payroll than you've got cities on this planet! They'll tie everything up nice and tight so that by the time the GCA forces get here, whatever happens will have happened. And possession is still nine-tenths of the law, even in a universe governed by lawyers."

"Fuck." It didn't matter who said it, they were all thinking it.

Mardon hissed out a breath between his teeth. "What do you want me to do, Tok? Help with security layers on the local network systems? Hack into the intership comms? Facilitate the evacuations?"

Irav shook his head and a strange look came into his black eyes. A last desperate hope—almost spiritual in nature. "I know what you've been doing with the Miner's Union, Kaen. I've let it go on because I once heard the voices too. I know there's something special about Lithos I and it's not just because it's home. We've got to protect that." Steel entered Irav Tok's demeanor and Mardon sat up straighter in response, at least, as straight as he could with a woman still wrapped around his cock. "I want you to seal off the mine, Mardon."

Mardon gave an inarticulate shout but Irav held up a commanding hand for silence. "We've got to protect whatever is down there. Someday, we'll get control back from the fucking Qsakians and we'll dig it out and figure out what the hell lives in the rock. But it's been eight thousand years and we still haven't figured it out. A mystery that old can wait a few more years, no matter how painful it is. But we can't let the Qsakians rape the place before we do solve that mystery."

Mardon merely gave a quick nod, which Irav returned before the signal blinked out, leaving Mardon and Galita in heavy silence.

"Men! You and your stoic silences. Are you really going to let that big hulk make you blow up the mines?" Galita twisted around to look him in the face and her wriggling was torturing his confused cock. His brain wanted to run through every possible solution to the enormous problem looming over him. His gut wanted to make damn sure Galita was safely on her way out of the system on the fastest ship he could steal. His cock just wanted to finish what they had been doing before the outside world had intruded.

Without conscious thought, his hips thrust against hers, his cock swelling back to full salute before he could try to rein it in and return to sanity. And really, he couldn't blame the poor thing. Being inside such a scorching, welcoming pussy and not getting to play properly—it was inhumane! Even the apparent end of the world couldn't get the blood pumping from his cock and back to Mardon's brain.

But Galita seemed to be in a similar state of confusion, her hips moving against him in tiny little circles, her nails scraping against the sides of his thighs, silently begging even as she railed against him. "You don't know that caving in the mine won't kill whatever is in there? Or send it into hiding for the next million years or so." She moaned slightly as he snapped his hips suddenly upward.

"An intelligence like this…" she began to pant, unable to keep up the flow of conversation without pauses which he punctuated by pinching her nipples or biting the soft skin on the side of her neck.

"Is completely unknown…" She leaned forward moving back onto hands and knees. He followed, his cock leading the way. "And could earn Lithos I special status with the GCA."

He grunted, pushing back analysis until the demands of his aching cock were satisfied. He gripped her hips and began a hard thrust, relishing the sound of her eager whimpers and the steady rhythm she kept up by pushing back against him. It felt so damn good inside her that he didn't want it to end, even though part of him was desperate for release. Another part was seriously considering the idea of curling up inside the hot, tight pussy that surrounded him like a sensuous glove and spending the next century or so in bliss.

Then he saw her hand sneak under her to tease her own clit and white heat coiled in his balls, demanding to explode out. Licking his thumb, he teased the outside of her rosebud anus with it.

"Oh, fuck. Yes!" she screamed in response. He slid his thumb inside slowly, feeling his own cock throbbing on the other side of her thin inner wall. She squirmed beneath him, lost in the throes of overwhelming stimulation. He wasn't too far behind. One more hard thrust of his hips and the walls rang with her blissful yells and that white fire erupted out of his cock and up his spine, flashing before his eyes in a blinding orgasm.

He didn't remember falling over her, he only remembered coming back to awareness with her body pinned under his, the soft exhalation of her sweet breath coming out in a soft giggle. "I didn't know talking about lawyers could get you so worked up."

He kissed her shoulder. "There's a lot you don't know about me, love. But we'll find out more. After we save the mines."

She nodded and sighed and he rolled off her, surprised at how weak his knees felt under him. When she stood up, her knees went out completely and she sat down hard on the couch, another blush staining her cheeks.

He laughed briefly, proud of himself but worried for her at the same time. Just how long had it been for her? He bent down and with more bravado than strength, swung her up into his arms, one arm under her knees and the other gripping her waist. She squealed as he carried her through the house to his bedroom. He was in search of clothes suitable for returning to the mines but the combination of warm willing woman and soft, inviting bed was almost too much to resist.

"I know what you are thinking and although my mind is willing I think we'd better give my symbiotes some time to repair my body. You're a big boy, you know that?"

If his skin was less dark, he would have blushed. Still he threw her down on the bed and bent over her, pulling one of her nipples into his mouth for a quick suck before releasing her with a pop. She mewed in protest and he smiled smugly before turning to his closet to find pants and a heavy shirt to negotiate the mines.

"I think I have a belt you could use to hold up some pants." Who was he kidding, his clothes would be huge on her. But still, it would be strangely satisfying to have her wearing his clothes.

"I'll be fine."

Of course, having her naked worked well too. It would just be damn hard to concentrate. But then again, having her there with him, live, nude, evidence of what he would stand to lose if the mines weren't there to hold her interest, maybe that would make his thoughts all the more clear.

"Whatever you wish, my dear." In a few moments he was dressed and before she could protest he'd scooped her back into his arms. "Your chariot awaits."

* * * * *

He took the sled all the way down into the canyon, bypassing its safety protocols for the sake of speed. He liked the casual way she had her arms around his waist and he wished that he too had forgone clothes so that he could feel her breasts pressed against his back as she clung to him just a little bit tighter on the turns.

She hopped off the gravsled and managed to keep her balance. He reached out to take her elbow but she gave him a look that clearly said she could fend for herself. He smiled, pleased that he'd done no permanent damage yet still just a little too proud of himself that she'd been so affected. He felt honored in a way. He knew from her profile that she preferred online sexual encounters to real-life ones, but he had no idea that the ratio was so small to make her tight enough to be a virgin. He wasn't sure that he'd ever be able to forget the feel of her so tight around his cock.

She walked toward the entrance with careful steps and although his mind should be whirring with plans to conceal the entrance with as little damage as possible, his thoughts were squarely occupied with watching the sway of her beautiful ass. How could he be so obsessed? He'd had her... Hell, he'd had her so hard even his own legs were shaky. Usually, a woman was out of his system after a couple of fucks. He'd had a few long-term relationships with women he'd had a lot in common with, but he had yet to hold a complete conversation with Galita Serhadze. He knew her file, he knew her mind from psych testing. And he knew she would feel betrayed that he knew so much about her while she was left in the dark about him. He couldn't tell her how he knew that they would meld like a perfect alloy, making something stronger together than they would be apart.

But she couldn't know that. She was only flying by instinct.

Fortunately, her instincts seemed honed pretty fine. She stopped at the small stand of avocado trees and stood on tiptoe to carefully squeeze one blue-black skinned fruit after another. Watching a naked woman caress fleshy sacks with a firm hand made his mouth go dry and his cock jump to attention yet again. He felt like a fucking hormonal kid, ready to hump until his eyes crossed and his cock was raw.

Work, you dumb lump. It's the goddamn end of the world. Don't worry about getting pussy, even if it's the tastiest pussy you've had in a century.

Shaking himself he strode forward, restraining himself from reaching for her hand as they walked side by side into the mines. The air here was so charged, his control so thin, that if he touched her he wouldn't be able to control himself — planetary welfare be damned.

* * * * *

Interlude

Jov Myrna emptied a trash receptacle into the heaving mass of stinking filth that was the compressor before the incinerator fired. This wasn't a job for a man, it was a job for a mech and a dumb mech at that. But the fucking Qsakian Syndicate boss in charge of this job was so shitfaced paranoid, he wouldn't let remote-controlled or high functioning mechs on his ship — afraid that he was being spied on.

So Jov — being pretty much a useless lump of flesh who claimed some expertise about Lithos, a planet he'd tried to rape but that he'd never set foot on — got to collect and dispose of the waste on the ship until they finally got into the Lithian system. Jov was pretty sure that he'd better come up with some pretty convincing shit to tell these trigger-happy bastards when they got into orbit, or he'd be holier than a *snolk* cheese from Fardo.

Juud was shoved aside, out on one of the six other ships sent to mount an attack on Lithos to force a hostile takeover of HLL Conglomerate and their holdings. The lawyers were prepping their end of things but possession was still nine-tenths of the law and the Syndicate had some very powerful people in the GCA who would look the other way to a little collateral damage in a newly transferred holding. And if HLL was sporting some super-secret offensive weaponry, then the surviving Board members had better keep quiet than risk a GCA investigation and the lock down and sanctions that might result.

Jov was rather excited about the whole thing. Maybe, just maybe, that *tralc* cunt Matrissa and all her friends were still lolling about in the lap of Lithian luxury and he'd still manage to catch a piece of prime tail before they got shipped off to the Karogian slave pits. Oh yes, HLL would be torn to pieces by the Syndicate and people could be bought and sold too...at least that was what some of the talkers in the mess crowed about. Jov was in the door to a whole new kind of existence, one where every rule could be twisted and everything was possible.

He was actually scared shitless. He wanted his nice cushy navigator's seat back. Even if he was shit at the job, at least he didn't have to unload other people's shit and spit. At least the captain of DMTR didn't randomly shoot crew members on a weekly basis. Fuck, he wanted *off* this piece of crap ship and out of this piece of crap life. Matrissa was one sweet piece of tail. A threesome with her and her friend Galita the Tessnet queen was still a star of his nightly fantasies. But fucking either of them until they bled or begged was not worth the constant worry that he was going to be the next to tick off Captain Tengmi.

But it was too late now—he hadn't been able to quietly disappear anywhere in the Qsakian system, where every atom of breathable air was wholly owned by the Qsakian Syndicate. He'd have been spaced faster than he could sneeze if he'd taken a step out of line. So now he was part of the Syndicate, with room and board if no pay and part of an invasion force for that cesspit, Lithos.

It was pretty damned funny how Tengmi and Juud and all the high muckity-fuckers were all wet and horny over Lithos and her superweapons, when the truth of it was mostly a bunch of bullshit he'd fed them. Lithos had some kind of secret, 'cause that pirate plague had been pretty ugly and folks got better too damn fast, but he'd bet his left nut that whatever the secret was, it wasn't some kind of big fucking gun or fancy-shmancy new shielding. He'd probably be dead then but at least the Qsakians would be eating a pile of shit and be tied up with the GCA for a couple decades and not much richer for the effort.

Jov Myrna almost felt sorry for Lithos. Almost.

Chapter Five
One Misstep

༄

Her skin itched. It always did when she went deep blue. Really, she shouldn't have cared about being caught in the throes of passion but her body reacted instinctively to hide — and now her skin was still a bluish shade as her system worked to remove the intense blue color from all her color cells from shoulders to knees. That's part of the reason she went nude on this journey — she wanted to make sure that her skin was returning to normal, even with the new symbiotes integrated into her body. So far, the symbiotes seemed to be nothing but helpful but she'd pushed her system to the max, between bouts of hard sex and a concealment reaction, so she wanted to make sure that all was well with her body if her mind would have to travel through raw veins of copper that traced like delicate filigree through the mines of Risheva.

She felt truly bared here. Now, she wished she had taken Mardon up on the offer of more rugged clothes, or any clothes at all. It wasn't the scrapes and bumps inevitable in scrambling over rocks and bending to enter low tunnels, it was the pulsing zing in the air, the energy rushing directly through her naked flesh.

She sighed and cradled the ripe avocadoes in her hands, feeling suddenly foolish for bringing them. But she had to try to replicate the situation of that initial experience as closely as possible. The coppery lushness of the blue fruit, the desire throbbing in her, all of it needed to be there. Now, she had all of that combined with a certain desperation to make contact and rescue this intelligence from oncoming doom.

She was amazed that she'd ever found her way out when she'd run the first time, the twists and turns of the tunnels seemed too intricate to follow now. Mardon radiated an intensity that was compelling sexy. *Infinity, I am addicted*! Her legs were still weak from the ride he'd given her earlier but her blood sang at the thought of the hard thighs hidden under heavy trousers and the cock that could make her practically blind with pleasure.

Trying to put her thoughts in order, she listened, ignoring the sound of footsteps and the whoosh of their breaths, vowing to hear nothing but the sounds of the mines. The faraway rush of the river echoed softly off the sandstone walls but as they descended into the hot depths of the mine, the sounds grew less and less until only the soft groaning of Lithos I could be detected. The planet, like every habitable planet, was almost alive — moving and shifting all the time, ready to birth new life or cause catastrophe once its ancient processes played themselves out.

Lithos was a mystery. One that deserved her full attention. She couldn't afford to be distracted by the hope that Mardon would reach out and take her hand, that his thigh would brush hers, that he would push her up against the nearest wall and fuck her until she was deaf from her own screams echoing in these magical caves.

The voice of the planet was trying to speak. Why did she have to be too damn horny to hear it!

"So," she broke the heavy silence, her insatiable curiosity unable to rest for long. "Why me?"

He stilled for a moment, a tension evident in his broad shoulders. It was only that one moment but she wondered at the weight of the question. "Why not you?" he tried to be flippant but fell flat in the attempt.

"Then why not any of the other five hundred InfoEngs on Lithos?"

He didn't answer and she huffed in annoyance. *Men*.

"Let's see, what's different about me? I'm young. There is an InfoEng on Lithos two Terran months younger than I am though and another a full year and a half younger."

"Both of those dolts are still wet behind the ears! Jarvik practically walks into walls he's on the net so much."

She wouldn't let him divert her with humor, even though that bright white smile was very distracting. And the tiny bit of defensiveness was endearing—another chink in the unreadable armor of Senior Engineer Mardon Kaen. He continued walking and she followed, continuing her interrogation.

"Then I am female. There's two hundred and twenty-three female InfoEngs registered on Lithos. Not counting the three hermaphrodites, in a class of their own, of course. So, my gender isn't it. Or is it?" He turned to look at her again, a wrinkle in his brow. With a deliberate shimmy she sent her breasts jiggling. He swallowed sharply, his eyes widening in response and she laughed loudly. The sounds cascaded and rippled through the tunnels, growing louder and louder until it seemed like the world laughed with her.

The sound did fade and silence descended as they stared at each other, both realizing that there was no way in hell all of that sound had been caused by her laughter alone. The mines themselves, or whatever presence lingered here, had taken up the sound of her wry amusement and magnified it a hundredfold.

"That!" Mardon whispered, a mixture of awe and a bit of jealousy in his voice. "That is why I contacted you, Galita Serhadze of the Genship DMTR." His eyes burned with that magical turquoise-blue as he spoke and fire coiled in her pussy at the passion he put on rampant display. Her muscles ached with the fucking he'd given her and the memories seared into her. And she could barely wait to make more.

Those eyes pinned her more effectively than pulse restraints ever could. He continued on, stepping closer and closer to her until her hard nipples brushed the fabric of his shirt. She wanted it to be the impressive chest beneath and her hands curled, the nails digging into her palms to restrain herself from reaching out to rip the fabric from his body. His voice washed over her like a physical touch. "I have taken every InfoEng I could convince to the Mines of Risheva in the decades since the mines awoke again. All of them feel something, many join the Miners' Union and vow to protect and investigate the mines, but no one has been able to decipher the signals within the copper. I saw what you could do in your tests on Mars and your record is beyond impressive. You could have your pick of the choicest jobs in the galaxy but you like the community on DMTR and the constant movement of a genship. You have seen more and experienced more than most Lithian Infotechs have in life spans three times as long...and you are naturally empathic, a condition very rare since the ravages of the psiwars. Therefore..."

"How the hell do you know all that?" It came out in the softest whisper but the rage in her voice was crystal clear. The avocadoes she held in her hands fell with a squishy plop as she lost the will to hold them, shock overwhelming all else.

He must have realized his mistake, because those blue eyes shut tight and pain washed across his face. "I'm sorry... I didn't..."

The words wouldn't come. She filled in the blanks. "Either you broke into the most protected computer system in the known galaxy, or you are..."

"An examiner for the Information Department on Mars, yes. I was one of your examiners."

She breathed in deeply and tried to keep in the scream that was building within her brain. He knew everything about her. Her worst fears. Her greatest joys. Her most embarrassing memories. He'd had access to almost every piece of information recorded in her forty-five years of life and all the intensive testing she'd endured to get her implants and her license to be a practicing Information Engineer.

She couldn't think right now. She didn't want to talk — she wanted to hit him. She certainly couldn't try to contact some kind of alien mind. Spinning around, she stalked back through the tunnels, intent on running away again.

"Galita, let me explain!" He wrenched her back around and instead of an explanation, crushed her lips with his, putting his soul into a kiss that surged down to her toes, emotion and passion overflowing into her tangled mind. It was too much, desire and anger, need and betrayal all swirling until she felt queasy with it.

He tore himself away. "I love you, Galita."

Her eyes widened in disbelief. She couldn't handle this. Too much too fast. She backed up, turned around and ran. She never saw the desolation on Mardon's face as she disappeared into the darkness.

* * * * *

Galita wasn't sure if she was lost because she didn't know her way, or lost because deep within she knew she couldn't run away and leave these mines in danger. If she wanted to, she could call up a visual recording of every move they had made in the last ten hours but she couldn't pull her mind into good enough order to make the effort worthwhile.

The warm darkness of the caves wasn't at all frightening. In fact, it was almost comforting. The subtle throbbing she'd felt from the first moment she'd set foot here seemed to change now, instead of calling out in question, the inaudible rhythm seemed to soothe her like a whispered lullaby at the edge of her perceptions. Following the smallest glimmer of light, she came out of one of the mine tunnels into a cave near the surface, lit from a skylight out to the planet's surface.

Beautiful didn't do the place justice. The walls were a warm red she immediately identified as the same color as Mardon's skin, no matter how much she wanted to push all thought of him away at the moment. The ancient digging equipment must have stopped in this place, because on one massive wall there was a mosaic of bright blue turquoise and veins of exposed raw copper covered with the green patina of age. Here and there, glimmers of severed quartz crystal refracted a hundred colors for a dash of sparkle. The beams of soft sunlight streaming into the cavern struck the surface of the rock and made every shade of color glow with lush warmth. Her legs gave out and she sat down hard, unable to hold back the tears any longer. Her scream of rage echoed through the room, bouncing around until soaring out into the sky.

Absently, she reached out toward the wall of exposed gems and scratched a fingernail through the light green patina over the copper, revealing the shimmering metal beneath. The throbbing from the entity within was magnified a hundredfold and seemed to enter her very blood, calming her like a mother's caress.

Her breath steadied, her pulse slowed. Her mind cleared so she could think. Briefly she tried to analyze the signal coming from the copper but it slipped away like a wriggling eel. She couldn't accomplish the cold process of Fourier transforms and signal processing when her mind was filled with longing and fear and deep vulnerability.

"What do you want?" the voice was familiar—the same voice that had called her from the Tessnet at that rave. Comforting, deep and alien. It wasn't a real voice, so much as a thought trickling through her mind like a life-giving stream.

The silence after rang through her, leaving her open and questioning. What did she want? How could she believe that Mardon loved her, when she barely knew the man? How could she believe that great sex—the only real sex she'd ever had—led her to return that love?

Into the swirling chaos of her thoughts, a message was received. Someone, somewhere was trying to send her a file. *What shitty timing*. She almost snorted and deleted the file out of hand but she realized the sender was Mardon. She pursed her lips. Was he sending her a love letter, or maybe a nasty revenge virus?

Come on, she knew he wasn't that petty. She opened the file—a massive file and found something completely unexpected.

His life. Every personal file over his century and a half of life. Something that not even a parent or a mate had access to, something that no other soul might ever see. From his birth records to his last psych exams, to the time he'd gotten a sled-parking ticket on Rdani III. Retina-captures of his most embarrassing moments. His dreams and his nightmares. The scent of his mother's special stew and the sound of his father's laugh. The embarrassment of his first kiss gone awry, when he'd managed to break the girl's nose. The intense and newly made memories of their coupling, the sensations he felt of the hot caress of her flesh around his cock and the awe he felt at the contentment on her flushed face afterward. She felt, deep in her soul, how much he truly did love her.

Tears poured down her face when she came back to herself. She didn't know how long she'd been lost in the datastream, only that she knew him now. And he was exactly what her instinct had always told her—a dynamic, passionate man with nothing to hide and everything to give to the person he loved. The only thing she had to question now was how she could possibly deserve the love of such a man.

Her vision blurry, her soul raw, she stared at the sparkling wall of stone before her. With a thump, a piece of turquoise fell at her feet, shining a brilliant blue that could only occur through intensive polishing. A perfect glowing teardrop. There was no way that it could have happened completely naturally. If the mind within these caves could produce something like that, a gift to try to ease her suffering, what else could it be capable of?

Once again she raised a shaking hand and touched the exposed copper, to communicate her joy at newfound love and her fears of heartbreak. Like a live wire, a scintillating message communicated itself to her through the veins of the planet. Wordless, voiceless but clear as a bell.

Go to him.

She knew exactly how to communicate to this entity. She knew how to understand it.

Chapter Six
It ain't over 'til...

☙

He should be finding munitions experts. Or at the very least some stonetalkers to try to coax the opening of the mine into disappearing. Stonetalking usually took weeks though. He needed to do something in order to keep the fucking Qsakians from finding anything. But instead, Mardon was sitting on his stupid ass on the rugged floor of some random tunnel, letting his diode light source flicker into nothingness while he stared at the carved walls of the mineshaft.

He was an idiotic fuckup. He'd finally found the woman of his dreams and he'd managed to screw it up completely in less than twenty-four standard hours. It must be some kind of record.

Sure, he'd sent her his personal files. Files so private, so intimate, that hacking into them would be a crime punishable by seventy-five standard years in galactic prison. The frightening thing was, he hadn't even given the act a second thought, he trusted her beyond reason. And he'd probably never see her face-to-face again. Acting like some kind of stalker was not a good start to a relationship.

He slammed his fist against the wall, wanting the pain to jar him from his paralysis. But there was no pain. He'd struck a wide vein of pure copper surrounded by a rim of blue-green turquoise. The metal had been soft to the touch—like stone appeared after stonetalkers spent hours in communion with it. Something very special was happening. He stroked the patina over the metal and watched in the dim light as the surface seemed to ripple like water.

Perhaps he'd completely lost it now. After years of balancing a hundred different realities in cyberspace, one epic romantic disappointment and he was now officially insane. He suppressed the urge to laugh and gave in to another impulse instead.

He pressed his finger into the metal, thrusting his hand into the cool but pliable copper until he was embedded to the wrist. The thrum he always felt within his blood, the call of Lithos in his symbiotes, was magnified a thousand times. But in all the glorious rhythm surrounding him and the prickling awareness in the liquid metal caressing his skin, he could not yet find understanding. As always, when he touched the copper in these tunnels, he felt a profound sense of comfort and belonging and heard a whispering voice within his mind—but the sounds never coalesced into meaning. This time however, the sound was persistent, driving, full of a need to bridge the gap in understanding. Mardon filled with frustration and poured more and more of himself into the link, trying to will himself to comprehend, to push aside all the pain and anger and emotion and logically draw out the meaning Lithos was trying to communicate to him.

"It won't work you know." Galita's voice was soft but it thundered through his focused mind, leaving his concentration in splinters. Angry for half a moment at the interruption, he drew his hand from the wall and stared at her with harsh eyes. When his eyes refocused on her lovely face, anger drained out of him and he was filled only with a hollow sort of gratitude that she had returned. But an ember of hope remained within him, as he was a man unlikely to give up without fighting for something he craved so badly.

He cleared his throat. "What won't work?"

She stepped closer and he couldn't help but be distracted by her magnificently naked body. In the low light, her skin was an alluring array of shadows and light, colors ranging from a blushing lavender to a pale gold. The fire of her hair and the intensity of her eyes drew his gaze away from the perfect peaks of her nipples and the curve of her hips. She smiled softly and his heart beat a little faster in response.

"You're trying to talk to them, aren't you? To Lithos?"

He nodded and blinked his eyes once, trying to refocus his thoughts on the emergency happening up on the surface. It was too easy to imagine that they were enfolded and safe down here. There was a ship of violent criminals racing toward them at faster-than-light speed and it was imperative that he protect this conduit into the special nature of Lithos I. His fucking cock would have to stop filling his thoughts with the sound of Galita screaming in pleasure as he rammed into her.

She knelt in front of him and reached down to pick up the avocadoes that had fallen to the floor hours ago when she'd fled from him. The fruit she'd picked was so ripe, the skin burst at the scratch of her nails and the turquoise-colored flesh beneath oozed out. He watched in frozen hope as she climbed onto him, perching her firm ass on his knees as she broke open one of the fruits and coated her fingers with the unctuous goodness. She brought her fingers to his lips and he let his lips part, letting those delicate fingers slide into his mouth. He tasted the rich flavor of the avocado, the metallic tang of the copper and the sweet essence that was Galita all at once.

His hands circled her waist without his consciously moving them. She looked down at them and gave him a half-smile. "You're not forgiven, you know." He flinched very slightly and pulled away, only to have her slam her hand over one of his. "Not *completely* forgiven. But you will be, eventually." The half-smile became a full one and her face shone with it. He couldn't help but smile back.

She leaned closer and the tip of her tongue swept over his lips, removing a trace of avocado. She slid sticky fingers under the edge of his tunic and she whipped it over his head and returned to the light contact of their lips. He tried to deepen the contact into a kiss but she pulled back again. She yanked at the waistband of his trousers, unbuttoning everything until she held his cock in her hand.

Swallowing loudly, Mardon tried to think of something to say. "You got them? The files…" She again held her finger to his lips and he licked the avocado off them.

"I got them. You didn't have to…"

He gave the tip of one of her fingers a bite and shook his head. "You know I did. Would anything else have brought you back?"

She pursed her lips. "Well, I think I may have an answer on how to understand the voice we keep hearing. So, I would have come back anyway. But, I have to admit I would have been in a much nastier mood and would have not wanted to do what I think is going to be necessary." She slid forward on his thighs until his cock brushed against the fine hair covering her pussy. She was already considerably aroused, as the lips of her pussy were parted and she continued her slide until he was poised at the entrance to her sheath, the hot slick lips of her pussy embracing him.

He let out a breath he hadn't known he'd been holding. He wasn't imagining this, he wasn't lost in some sim he'd created in desperation. No sim ever felt as good as the melting sweet heat of Galita Serhadze. No sim could smell as intoxicating. No sim could smile with her eyes as she did.

"Aren't you the least bit interested in my answer, my love?" she pouted and he had to kiss her, fuck the world collapsing around them. His lips claimed hers in a scorching kiss of renewal and welcome, hunger and need. Lips and teeth and tongue danced, learning the contours of one another's pleasure and how perfectly they meshed. By the end of the kiss, when breathing became absolutely necessary, Mardon realized he was embedded within Galita balls-deep, her legs wrapped around his back.

Panting for breath, wanting to turn them over and slam into her properly, he restrained himself just enough to use the few remaining brain cells receiving blood supply. "So, what is your solution and what exactly do you need to do to accomplish communication with it?" He tensed the muscles of his ass, thrusting up into her slightly and making her moan—a sound he would never get enough of.

Then she growled, another sound he would live to hear more of. She gritted her teeth and closed her eyes, struggling to keep her thoughts in order. "The voice is a *them*, not an it. It's the planet, all the consciousness of the planet. Every plant and rock, every fish and insect. And it's us too...or it should be."

He stared at her. She was brilliant. It was a ridiculous answer, a revolutionary answer and yet it had to be right. He felt it in his very bones.

"The symbiotes in our blood are part of it too. It's the voice that calls us back to Lithos if we've been gone too long. The need to be part of the whole consciousness once again."

"Then why can only you hear so much—make some sense of it? And how do we tell it—them—of the coming danger?"

"I'm not certain but I think that I hear the symbiotes more, because they are so new for me. You've had them as part of you since birth...probably since conception. They are completely a part of you, so much you don't listen for them anymore. I do."

Again, her intellect, her instincts astonished him. He felt the overwhelming need to claim her as his own, if she would let him. "So, how do I help you speak with them?"

"I need to recreate what happened the first time I heard them—and I need to heighten the experience. I hope to be able to warn them if I...if we can."

He raised an eyebrow and she readjusted her position, causing pleasure to flash through him, distracting him away from disbelief. He'd spent decades trying to communicate with the entity within these caves. He doubted he would be able to do so now. But he believed that Galita could. "How does this," he thrust up again and she arched her neck as the muscles of her pussy clamped around him, driving him to the edge of sanity. "How does this help with communication?"

"I wanted you," she panted, "I wanted you very, very badly from the first moment I saw you in Aroll. You'd brought me here. You'd fed me avocado. I lusted after you so much I could barely see straight, and then I touched the raw copper and everything clicked. I could sense emotions, feel sensations I'd never dreamed of. But then desire took over and all I could do was act on it." She blushed, despite the fact that he was fully embedded within her, she was still blushing. *Infinity, she was gorgeous.*

"So, you think that if that desire is satisfied, you'll be able to talk?"

She shook her head, wisps of red hair dancing in the humid air of the mine. "No, I think that if we are joined, physically joined, that along with our symbiotes we might both be able to talk to them."

Hope surged, along with physical need. A love he never expected to find and she offered him the chance to fulfill a lifelong dream. Contact with a completely unique species…damn, a whole planetary consciousness! "Ok, so we've taken care of unfulfilled desire." He swept a hand down from her waist to stroke his thumb over her clit. She squeaked and he laughed. "Now, we need some more of that avocado…just to be certain."

He plucked the avocado from her hand and twisted it open, discarding the pit and coating his hands with the lush buttery flesh. She stared at him with those intense brown eyes and then let out a squeal as he clapped his hands over her breasts, smearing the oily pulp all over her. He could sense that her indignant shock was quickly replaced with desire once again as he carefully licked the brilliant blue-green paste off her breasts. Stroking his tongue with broad motions, the taste of her salty-sweet skin matched perfectly with the avocado. He sucked at her nipples and he could feel her quaking, the muscles of her pussy fluttering with her pleasure.

Then he felt the cold slap of his own medicine. She had filled a palm with more avocado and had smeared the cold goo onto the side of his neck. She followed this harsh treatment with the heat of her tongue, her teeth scraping against the sensitive skin on the side of his neck. His cock pulsed inside her and he gripped her hips, arching up into her, pulling her away and then slamming her down on to his cock.

She nipped at his ear. "Tsk-tsk. We have a mission to complete—have to wait to come, big boy."

He grumbled. His voice was hoarse and impatient. "What else, woman?"

She captured his hand in her own, both of them sticky with blue-green avocado. "Guide me, stone man. Guide us both into the rock." She spoke within his mind, bypassing the Tessnet and accessing his implants directly. She was within his mind and he could see within hers.

Together, they pressed against the copper vein, sliding into the metal with little resistance but with a welcoming pulse of energy. He heard Galita's intake of breath both out loud and within his mind. With her hand in his, this entrance into the lifeblood of Lithos was much easier. This time, Mardon didn't feel the troubling buzz of voices he couldn't understand. This time, he no longer felt so alone and lost.

What is happening? Why are the Ones leaving?

The voice echoed, layered as though a thousand voices whispered at once.

Galita seemed shocked into silence that her plan had worked. It was up to him to speak. "There is a danger coming. People who do not understand Lithos. People who want to abuse the planet."

Ones from the Black? Ones who came before learned to live with us. New Ones are learning as well. We feel them become part of the whole. These coming Ones are not the same?

Galita snapped out of her shock. "No, they are not. They care only to take from Lithos and not to add to its beauty. They will take and take, until they drain Lithos I dry."

When will the bad Ones come?

Mardon accessed the telemetry from the stealth satellite still operational in orbit. Most of the others had been moved into hiding on the moons. "They will arrive…"

This is us? Seen from the Black?

There was a sense of awe that pervaded his mind. Mardon realized that more than his own visual cortex was looking at the readouts from the satellite. Dozens, hundreds, perhaps thousands of eyes—compound, multifaceted, small and large, underwater and underground—all these eyes looked through his mind and out into the blackness of space. Down onto the surface of the planet, from mountains to plains, deserts to Lake Silith, bright sunside and dark blackside.

We are beautiful here from the Black.

The view refocused outward, toward the coming threat.

The specks moving so quickly…those are the bad Ones?

He felt disoriented, larger than himself when he answered. "They are entering orbit right now. The first landing parties will touch down within the hour."

We do not understand your measurements of time. It is all so fast—all of the Ones live so quickly. But we can be fast when it is needed.

Mardon gripped Galita's hand even harder, needing the touch of her hand, even within the metal. The grip of her sheath on his cock kept him sane, grounded. But together they were about to experience something amazing.

Deep in his belly, he felt a burning and it wasn't the fact that all he'd had to eat all day was licks of avocado from his lover. Part of him realized he was not feeling his own body— he was sensing the planet itself. Deep within Lithos I, the molten core of the planet shifted and moved with constant pulsing. But pushed into action, the planet rose up to protect itself. The core spun even faster, the circulating liquid rock surging in rushing torrents. The ground shook slightly as internal pressure rocketed to levels never measured in the ten thousand years mankind had inhabited Lithos I.

The first two ships entering orbit had no idea of the danger they were in. When they fired plasma shots at the remaining non-stealth satellites, Mardon felt his skin prickle—the only warning of what Lithos was preparing to do. The magnetic fields encircling the planet, shielding it from damaging particles from the sun, those fields depended upon the energy of the molten core. The increase in motion and pressure was reflected in those magnetic fields. And the Qsakian ships, never expecting resistance to come from such an unexpected quarter, had no time to shield their sensitive electronics from the pulsing electromagnetic wave that hit them.

The shielded satellite shook under the stress, its visuals quaking and sparking. But Mardon didn't have to see what was going on. With new strange senses he could feel the two ships in orbit being shaken by the rapidly shifting magnetic fields, inertial dampeners doing nothing to prevent the contents of both ships being hurled from side to side.

The ships struggled out of orbit, limping away from Lithos. The other ships sent off a couple of stray shots but they fell far short of doing any damage and looked rather pathetic in view of their retreat. Mardon felt his blood surge in victory and Galita's excitement as she bobbed up and down, making him remember once again that he was buried deep inside this sweet woman. Just was he was about to loose his grip on logical thought and begin pounding into her once again, he saw a distinctive red and black ship came into view.

More bad Ones?

"No!" Galita screamed inside his head. "That's a GCA ship! Don't attack, they've come to help."

Mardon thought they had probably just come to make sure that carnage was kept to a prescribed minimum but regardless, it would do no good to have the planet attack the GCA. Lawyers didn't take kindly to that sort of thing.

The prickling along his skin lessened but the roiling heat within him began to escalate. He felt more than heard Galita moan and he knew she felt the same way.

Acting as quickly as Ones is difficult. Pressure builds up in the core and must find release.

Mardon knew on some level that Lithos was volcanic and that the boiling magma that had been stirred into a frenzy would bubble up to the surface. But most of his mind was consumed with the way his body felt. All of the heat of a planet was now centered on where his cock brushed in tiny motions through the slick pussy of his lover. Galita clutched his ass with her free hand, pulling herself against him until he was so deep inside her he touched her cervix. She let out a soft sigh and suddenly he had to thrust, he had to reach completion within her.

Without rational thought, he pulled their entwined hands from the copper and pushed her back, somehow managing to unfold his legs and press her down into the rough floor without losing their connection. Immediately, her supple arms and legs wrapped around him, pulling him to her body with desperation equal to his own.

"Fuck me!" she hissed in his ear. "Please."

"As you wish," he managed to growl out. Holding himself over her, staring down into brown eyes that seemed to flash with fire, he pounded into her, determined to make her come before releasing the explosion inside him.

He didn't notice the rumbling of the earth. He couldn't have known of the smoke pouring out of a dormant volcano on the blackside. Mardon could think of nothing but the slide of his cock in her sweet sheath, the feel of her breasts crushed against his chest, the sound of her pants and moans as he hit just the right spot to make her shake.

The pressure built and built until it could no longer be contained. He roared his orgasm as she screamed in bliss and on the other side of the planet, a volcano spewed out a spectacular display of molten lava.

* * * * *

They walked into Mardon's house hand in hand, silent and contemplative in the closeness they had shared with each other and a planet. They were not prepared to see the towering black frame of Irav Tok standing in the atrium looking pissed.

"Warning, Kaen. Next time, I want some warning if you are going to call up geologic forces on command in front of the Galactic Corporate Attorneys!"

Mardon opened his mouth to retort but Galita beat him to the punch. "How the hell were we supposed to warn you of that! You told us the GCA wouldn't come for weeks. And we just saved this planet, well...the planet saved itself but..."

Irav threw back his head and laughed loud enough to set the crylic windows shaking. "Don't mind me, woman. I'm just here to say thank you and avoid the GCA rep for an hour or two. You do realize that you'll have to repeat some of that or the lawyers will bury us in red tape and quarantine..."

Galita clutched Mardon's hand and Mardon could feel her blush hard.

"Tok, it's not that easy to replicate...in public."

Irav raised an eyebrow and took in Galita's brilliant complexion. He snorted in laughter. "Ha and I used to think you were a cold fish, Mardon."

"Same to you Irav. But then again, Ivani Gorl got herself a fish and he seems to have melted her down quite a bit."

"True! Hell, without her pulling strings with the GCA, they'd have never been here to 'observe' in the first place. And since they witnessed the whole thing, they know that the Qsakians fired the first shot."

The wall screen flared to life in the living room and a larger than life image of a very pregnant, mostly naked, very angry Matrissa Prospera stared hard at them.

"Irav Tok, what the hell are you doing in Risheva!"

Irav remained silently blinking at his wife. Matrissa looked distinctly uncomfortable, one hand pressing against her back while the surface of her stomach swirled with movement and color in a nauseating kaleidoscope. "This little fellow would insist on arriving when the planet is in utter confusion and all the physicians are trying to assist in evacuations." Her eyes clenched shut as her teeth bared in a feral grimace when another contraction hit. "Irav! You get back here and into this fucking basement bunker before I pop out your son alone with this cold medtech machine for company, or I will personally make certain I fry up your balls for my next breakfast!"

Her eyes popped open and shone with gazed pain and the ferocious anger only hormonal females were capable of. Irav swallowed and sprinted out the door to the nearest gravsled and sped off toward the closest tunnel car to get him home.

Mardon doubled over laughing but Galita slapped him hard on the ass. "Don't laugh at a woman in labor. It's bad luck, you never know what might happen to you!"

"I wasn't laughing at her. I was laughing at him."

"Don't you think you would be just as frantic, my love?"

He just smiled at her and drew her in for a kiss. "When the time comes, I'm sure I will be."

*****

Interlude

Jov Myrna was pretty damn banged up. In fact, he hadn't yet realized that he'd lost one of his legs as a massive storage bin had landed on him. His lack of comprehension of his state was instead due to the profusely bleeding wound on his head from being tossed back and forth across the cargo bay.

He wasn't sure what the hell had happened but he knew that somehow, those damned Lithians had escaped his Qsakian masters. The ship was lurching along into hyperdrive with some fucked up noises that sounded like the ship was about to tear itself in two. At least, if Jov died that way, the rest of the Qsakian motherfuckers who'd dragged him into this pile of shit situation would die a nasty death too.

DMTR didn't look so bad anymore, compared to life as a trashman for Qsakians. As he lost consciousness, he cursed at Lithos. He cursed at DMTR. He ranted against Matrissa Prospera and all her friends. But most of all, he cursed at himself.

Epilogue
An encore

ත

Stretched out across the massive expanse of their bed, Galita smiled a lazy grin of contentment. Naked except for the turquoise teardrop hanging on a chain around her neck, she stretched the sleep from her muscles. With a thought directed at the remote control node of the room, the heavy blackout shades lifted, revealing the clear crylic wall that looked out across the Risheva plains. The surface of Lithos I was never without the soft orange light that the star sent out and the red rocks and greens and grays of the trees and bushes always seemed ready to be lovingly painted. Lithos was truly blessed with beauty.

Mardon let out a soft groan, rolling over and securing an arm around her waist, pulling her against him with firm command. Giving a satisfied grunt he settled back into the soft bed with the obvious intention of falling back into sleep. Galita was not letting him off so easily.

Her body was already humming with want again. She used to be able to go three or four months without engaging in a Tessnet sex rendezvous. She had no idea her desire could be so potent and so demanding. She couldn't go more than a few hours without needing his touch or the satisfying slide of his cock inside her. Usually, he was very accommodating.

It had only been two months since Lithos I had chased away the Qsakians. In that time, Mardon and she had helped to demonstrate to the GCA the special nature of the planet. Fortunately, contact now required a much less…intimate connection between individuals for an understanding to be established. Accordingly, the GCA has awarded Lithos special protected status available only to sentient beings. No agency could perform a hostile takeover of the planet without obtaining the express approval of the native species—Lithos itself.

She and Mardon had become virtually inseparable. Physical contact—just the brush of a hand or playing footsie beneath a table, seemed necessary to her equilibrium now. She'd never thought she'd be the type to find a mate, yet it was obvious to both of them they were meant to be.

The only problem so far—he was not a morning person. She had to be creative to get him to wake up.

"So, Matrissa tells me that you Lithians can do something very interesting with clay. Irav can make a copy of himself that can...ahem, participate in the bedroom in interesting ways."

He turned his face toward her and one eyebrow arched, even though his eyes remained stubbornly shut.

"She actually managed to talk about something other than the baby?"

Galita snorted in frustration. "Yes, the last week she's talked about nothing but sex. With a natural birth, they couldn't do a thing for weeks and..."

"Trust me, Galita, I don't want to know anything about Irav Tok's sex life, or lack thereof." His eye cracked open. "And I'm sorry to disappoint but I can't sculpt anything except mountains of mashed Ryvan tubers."

She let out an exaggerated sigh of disappointment. *It sure had sounded interesting.* She closed her eyes, preparing her next angle of attack, when she felt Mardon's weight settle on top of her, his cock half hard against her stomach. She opened her eyes to see him hovering above her, his blue eyes wide awake and alight with challenge. She repressed her smile of victory. Sometimes, you had to let a man think he had won in order to get optimum performance.

"I may not be able to replicate myself in blood and clay but I have other skills you might appreciate."

Galita purred as his hips rolled against hers, his cock brushing against the trimmed hair of her pussy and teasing her swollen lips. She didn't care what the hell Mardon was planning, as long as she could feel the thrill of penetration before the wanting became painful. The man had entirely too much fun teasing her.

"What's your pleasure, my little spitfire?" His eyes grew slightly unfocused, half in the moment with her and half into Tessnet trance. And part of her was dragged with him into fantasy. She was still in the bed, still anticipating the thrust of his cock down into her pussy. But she was also standing at the window, completely exposed, her legs spread wide, her sweating hands pressed against the crylic wall. From behind, his hands were on her hips, digging into her skin. His rock-hard erection was a scant cetar within her and she needed him deeper — much deeper. She mewed with impatience.

She was on the floor next to the bed. He knelt over her, his ass just above her chest, his hands gripping a bedpost and his cock sliding past her lips and she clutched his powerful thighs on either side of her shoulders.

Up against the door, her legs hooked over his elbows, his cock about to impale her as she strained against the wall, aching for him to fuck her already.

She sat on his lap, his hands gripping her ass as she began the slow slide down that thick cock. This chair was absolutely the perfect height, giving her balance and control to tease him as badly as he teased her.

She knelt on the bed, the firm cheeks of her ass high in the air. She bit her lip as his fingers teased the sensitive skin of her ass, making sure she was relaxed and ready for him to fill her to bursting. Anticipation ran hot through her veins and her stomach clenched with need.

The tip of his tongue circled her clit, getting close, so damn close but not giving her what she needed. His fingers circled the entrance to her pussy. One, two, three long fingers played at thrusting but never coming all the way in. She was spread out across the bed, clutching at the sheets as he knelt on the floor, her legs over his wide shoulders. Those blue-green eyes looked up at her with desire and challenge and more than a little mischief.

Holy fuck. Just when she thought she knew the talents of Mardon Kaen, the man creates seven full sims on top of physical movement of his own body and hers. Eight couples, poised for completion and all of the sensations running through the two of them.

"Is this interesting enough for you, my little Phytos?"

Galita couldn't marshal the words to respond. She'd never heard of a human who could maintain more than three sims at a time without going insane. But seven? Forget her sanity, she wasn't even sure she would be able to survive the experience. But what a way to die.

One of the sims angled her hips just so and it was an irresistible temptation for one of him. Then a cry of satisfaction magnified sixteen times, the moment of hesitation ended and the sweet slap of flesh on flesh began.

Galita was completely full, more open and more raw than she would have thought possible. He filled her in every way possible and she couldn't think, could barely react. She could only feel. And feel. And feel.

From every angle and every position she felt the scrape of nails on skin, the slap of a hand on her ass, the whisper of heavy breathing in her ear. The scent of sex surrounded them, all of them.

Each incarnation was writhing, skin in shades of green and blue, calm florals and crazy geometrics and that coppery lace that Mardon seemed to have developed a distinct fondness for. But always, the earthy redness of Mardon's skin grounded hers, kept her from splintering in a thousand directions as sensation flooded every neuron and synapse over and over again.

His voice was harsh, unrestrained in her ear as he struggled to maintain a vestige of control. "Is this interesting enough for you, Galita?"

She could only exhale and gasp in another giant breath. The chair creaked as she thrust down on his cock, trying to get the perfect angle. Her back arched as she was pounded into the door, the opening mechanism whirring in confusion as Mardon thumped powerfully into her over and over again. Her hands frustratingly slipped down the crylic window as she tried to keep steady in precisely the position that made lights flash before her eyes as he slammed into her.

The sims grew closer and closer, until hands and lips, pussies and cocks were everywhere. Long fingers thrust into her sheath as she swallowed his cock. His tongue circled her clit as his teeth scraped along one nipple. She looked down in wonderful confusion to see Mardon staring at her from attending to one breast and her own eyes smiling mischievously back at her from the other sensitive nipple.

The faces looking up at her then stopped their attentions to her aching breasts and engaged in a deep kiss that she could feel to the tips of her toes — hot, wet and primal. She was kissing Mardon. Or was she kissing herself? Or was that Mardon kissing Mardon?

Some version of her whimpered with desperation. It was too damn much! A cock hit her G-spot over and over again, while another filled her from behind and that talented tongue sucked her clit with exquisitely light pressure.

The orgasms started to ripple like earthquakes, signaling a warning before the oncoming tidal wave. She shuddered with each climax, sucking and licking, thrusting and scratching and rolling her hips in time with the rhythm of ecstasy surrounding them.

She was intent on the friction of that cock sliding within her, gripping that hardness with every ounce of her strength, demanding he give her everything.

She was trying her best not to explode, her balls tight as the white-hot release coiled at the base of her...his...her spine? The tightness of the pussy gripping her was unbearably sweet.

All the barriers had fallen. Pleasure spiraled outward until it was impossible to tell where she began or ended. The twisting, throbbing, sweat-slick mass began to erupt into one giant orgasm. She lost track of which sim was screaming, which pussy was throbbing, which orifice cum was spurting into which, with hot waves.

"Is this interesting..."

"YES! Damn you stubborn man, YES!"

The last thing she saw before her brain was lost to a white wall of bliss were those intense turquoise-blue eyes hovering above her. Then she ceased to exist.

The universe was a beautiful thing when nothing but pleasure throbbed within. No day or night or worries or thoughts to plague a being. No name or identity to protect with pride or arrogance. Nothing to lose and no way to hurt. Most of all, there was no loneliness. He was here. Entwined with her in the white.

His presence reminded her to breathe. She still couldn't remember her name though. Just as she began to panic, to realize she was lost in the ether of consciousness, the low thrum called her back. The soft pounding of blood in her veins, the harsh panting of her breath, the delicious ache in her muscles. The weight of the man on top of her.

A whisper drew her back together, all the parts that had shattered upon impact with that wall of brilliant ecstasy. The Lithos in her blood, the symbiotes that were a part of the planet, pulled her consciousness back into some semblance of order.

A low laugh completed the process. "That was...that was..."

"Very interesting." Her voice was so low and rough from the screams Mardon had wrung from her that she couldn't recognize it.

They were still so closely entwined mentally and physically she could read his thoughts. He was worried about her, afraid that she'd been lost to him.

"Don't worry, love. You brought me back safe and sound." She smiled at him, reaching up to push a stray red strand of hair from those luminous eyes of his.

He made a sound that was half grunt and half laugh. "I think you overestimate my powers, Galita. It was the symbiotes. They allow us, both of us, a more concrete tie to our physical bodies. I would have never tried this otherwise."

She giggled provocatively. "I don't think I can ever, ever overestimate your 'powers' after that ride. I'm surprised that you don't have women lined up around your house, begging for a moment of your masterful attention."

He looked suddenly serious and leaned down over her face, his weight on his elbows and the lithe length of his body pressed against hers from toes to nose. "Do you honestly think I've done this with anyone else?"

She knew him. She knew him like no one else could. And she knew that she was the only one who had ever shared him so completely. "You know, it wasn't the symbiotes."

He arched an eyebrow at her and that lopsided smile tugged at her heart. He leaned done and kissed her softly, tugging her bruised bottom lip between his one with infinite tenderness. He pulled back just enough to let her whisper.

"It wasn't the symbiotes who brought me back to sanity. It was you, Mardon Kaen. You are my home and I'll always belong here."

His eyes grew impossibly bright and he returned for another, more passionate kiss that left her breathless once again.

"So, you said something about wanting to get up. Shall we?"

She pushed at his shoulder until he rolled over and then she snuggled into his shoulder with purpose. Exhaustion and comfort pulled her into the embrace of sleep, as Mardon's arms wrapped around her to complete her satisfaction. Yes, on this strange, wonderful planet, she had truly found her home.

Also by Amy Ruttan

༄

Love Thy Neighbor
Masque of Desire
Tantalizing Treats (*anthology*)

About the Author

Amy discovered her love of the written word when she realized that she could no longer act out the fantastical romances in her head with her dolls. Writing about delicious heroes was much more fun than playing with plastic men dolls with the inevitable flesh-colored "tighty whities".

She loves history, the paranormal, and will spew out historical facts like a volcano, much to her dearest hubby's chagrin.

When she's not thinking about the next sensual romp, she's chasing after two rug rats and reading anything spicy that she can get her hands on.

Amy welcomes comments from readers. You can find her website and email address on her author bio page at www.ellorascave.com.

Tell Us What You Think

We appreciate hearing reader opinions about our books. You can email us at Comments@EllorasCave.com.

Also by Regina Carlysle

☙

Breath of Magic
Elven Magic (*anthology*)
Killer Curves
Spanish Topaz
Tempting Tess

About the Author

Regina Carlysle is an award winning, multi-published author. She likes writing that is hot, edgy, and often humorous, and puts this trademark stamp on all of her stories. Regina lives in west Texas with her husband of 25 years and counting and is a doting, fawning, and over-indulgent mother to her two kids. When she's not penning steamy erotic tales or hot contemporary stories, she's indulging in long chats with friends who help her stay sane and keep her laughing.

Regina welcomes comments from readers. You can find her website and email address on her author bio page at www.ellorascave.com.

Tell Us What You Think

We appreciate hearing reader opinions about our books. You can email us at Comments@EllorasCave.com.

Also by Elaine Lowe

☙

Enchant the Dawn
Lady Six Sky
Nancy's Sweet Spelling Bee
Reveal the Heart
Scandalous Profession
Sea of Pearls
Seeds of Garnet

About the Author

෨

Elaine Lowe is a work-at-home mom in Silicon Valley California. Of her many part-time jobs, her favorite one by far is writing. She has a background in biotech, but she has branched out into the demanding world of home management, toddler entertainment, transcription, envelope stuffing, and of course, writing romantic and erotic fiction.

A love of history, magic and romance combines to inspire a lot of her writing. That and her wonderful husband, who is a fantastic sounding board, support system, and research consultant. He really enjoys research. And so does she.

Look for upcoming novels involving forces of nature, a touch of magic, and the idea that sensuality is not specific to any particular time period.

Elaine welcomes comments from readers. You can find her website and email address on her author bio page at www.ellorascave.com.

Tell Us What You Think

We appreciate hearing reader opinions about our books. You can email us at Comments@EllorasCave.com.

Why an electronic book?

We live in the Information Age—an exciting time in the history of human civilization, in which technology rules supreme and continues to progress in leaps and bounds every minute of every day. For a multitude of reasons, more and more avid literary fans are opting to purchase e-books instead of paper books. The question from those not yet initiated into the world of electronic reading is simply: *Why?*

1. ***Price.*** An electronic title at Ellora's Cave Publishing and Cerridwen Press runs anywhere from 40% to 75% less than the cover price of the exact same title in paperback format. Why? Basic mathematics and cost. It is less expensive to publish an e-book (no paper and printing, no warehousing and shipping) than it is to publish a paperback, so the savings are passed along to the consumer.
2. ***Space.*** Running out of room in your house for your books? That is one worry you will never have with electronic books. For a low one-time cost, you can purchase a handheld device specifically designed for e-reading. Many e-readers have large, convenient screens for viewing. Better yet, hundreds of titles can be stored within your new library—on a single microchip. There are a variety of e-readers from different manufacturers. You can also read e-books on your PC or laptop computer. (Please note that Ellora's Cave does not endorse any specific brands.

You can check our websites at www.ellorascave.com or www.cerridwenpress.com for information we make available to new consumers.)

3. ***Mobility.*** Because your new e-library consists of only a microchip within a small, easily transportable e-reader, your entire cache of books can be taken with you wherever you go.

4. ***Personal Viewing Preferences.*** Are the words you are currently reading too small? Too large? Too… ANNOYING? Paperback books cannot be modified according to personal preferences, but e-books can.

5. ***Instant Gratification.*** Is it the middle of the night and all the bookstores near you are closed? Are you tired of waiting days, sometimes weeks, for bookstores to ship the novels you bought? Ellora's Cave Publishing sells instantaneous downloads twenty-four hours a day, seven days a week, every day of the year. Our webstore is never closed. Our e-book delivery system is 100% automated, meaning your order is filled as soon as you pay for it.

Those are a few of the top reasons why electronic books are replacing paperbacks for many avid readers.

As always, Ellora's Cave and Cerridwen Press welcome your questions and comments. We invite you to email us at Comments@ellorascave.com or write to us directly at Ellora's Cave Publishing Inc., 1056 Home Avenue, Akron, OH 44310-3502.

Cerridwen, the Celtic Goddess of wisdom, was the muse who brought inspiration to storytellers and those in the creative arts. Cerridwen Press encompasses the best and most innovative stories in all genres of today's fiction. Visit our site and discover the newest titles by talented authors who still get inspired - much like the ancient storytellers did, once upon a time.

Cerridwen Press
www.cerridwenpress.com

Discover for yourself why readers can't get enough of the multiple award-winning publisher

Ellora's Cave.

Whether you prefer e-books or paperbacks,

be sure to visit EC on the web at
www.ellorascave.com

for an erotic reading experience that will leave you breathless.